LOVE'S RENEWAL

When Dani heard that Prentice
McCulloch meant to turn the old Manor
into a country club for his smart-set
friends she decided to fight him. But
Prentice seemed determined to win her
over . . .

LOVE'S RENEWAL

BY

SARA FRANCIS

MILLS & BOON LIMITED
ETON HOUSE   18–24 PARADISE ROAD
RICHMOND   SURREY TW9 ISR

MILLS & BOON and Rose Device is registered in U.S. Patent and Trademark Office

First published in Great Britain 1987 by Mills & Boon Limited

© Sara Francis 1983

Australian copyright 1983

ISBN 0 263 11455 4

Set in Baskerville 10½ on 11½ pt. 07–0787

Printed and bound in Great Britain by Collins, Glasgow

For
Stephen
and for
Christopher and Susannah
with love

CHAPTER ONE

'DANI, will you please keep your head still?'

Dani Robertson sighed and wished that she dared to raise her right hand and ease the ache in her neck. This was the third time she had been rebuked and Brian's voice was now betraying his irritation.

'I can't stay much longer.' She mumbled the words as she tried to keep her lips still. 'I'm going to Marina's for dinner.' Marina was her sister.

'You've only been here for an hour. If I'd known you were such a fidget, I'd never have asked you to sit for me.'

Dani considered an answer to this blunt statement but decided not to annoy the man any more. The pose that she had been told to adopt when she had started sitting for this portrait had seemed quite comfortable at first, but now she was acutely aware of every muscle and nerve in the top half of her body. She had explored with her eyes the part of the studio within her limited vision over and over again, and now she was becoming restless.

She could just see Brian out of the corner of her eye. Tall, broad, with very white teeth emphasised by his thick black beard, he was the epitome of an artist; untidy, both in himself and his home, given to fits of moodiness that he airily put down to temperament, forgetful and casual. His eccentricity, Dani was sure, was deliberately fostered, but his painting was good.

'Why did you ask me to sit for you?' It was an idle

question and she expected him to retort that she should not fish for compliments.

'You've got an interesting face.'

'Who, me?' She was unable to resist the surprised comment.

'Mmm.' Brian looked from the portrait to her and then back again. 'Good bone structure, beautiful eyes and a kind of fey look about you. Sometimes you look like a child and sometimes like a woman. I'm trying to capture something, and I'm not even sure what it is. Sometimes I see the exact expression I want, but it's gone before I can get it down on canvas.'

'Oh.' Dani could think of no appropriate comment and she felt colour steal into her face as she realised he must have studied her closely before asking her to sit for him, even to the extent of telling her to wear a certain dress. It was a simple blue one, high-necked with a neat collar, and a long-time favourite of hers.

'I don't know why you stay here,' Brian said suddenly, and Dani blinked as she tried to assimilate the change of subject.

'The way you bully me, neither do I.'

'I don't mean in this room, I mean in the village.'

Dani considered the statement for a moment. 'Why shouldn't I? Marina's here. It's a nice school and I like my infants. I like my flat, too . . . even if my landlord is a bad tempered old bear.' Brian was her landlord.

'You're too young to look on whist drives as your main source of entertainment.'

What Brian had said was essentially true, but Dani resented his somewhat acerbic tone. He was reminding her, not very subtly, that she was twenty-six years old without any particular ambitions.

'Are you saying that I'm boring?' she asked lightly.

'Boring? No, dear, just a little too old for your age, sometimes.'

'Thanks very much.'

Brian could be exasperating and Dani knew that nothing would please him more than a discussion about her life-style. She said nothing, deciding silently that she was not in the mood for home truths, and once again let her eyes wander over that part of the studio within her limited vision.

A big deal table held an array of brushes and palettes and paints. Despite the image of absent-minded untidiness that Brian liked to foster, there was nothing casual about his approach to his work. The palettes were clean and neatly stacked, the brushes arranged in order of size and the tubes of paint that he was not using all together in a box. The canvasses, Dani decided, were a little more untidy, but even here there was some semblance of logic. Larger, hardboard pictures supported smaller ones as they lay propped against the wall and a smaller pile of canvasses were a little apart from the others. In yet a third section, a few framed pictures lay awaiting their creator's attention.

Dani liked Brian's pictures, but she had watched the progress of her own portrait with mixed feelings. The steady grey eyes that stared back at her from the canvas, the neat, straight nose and the slightly curved mouth were all her features, unmistakably so, and yet she still felt that something was not quite right. Her own face seemed familiar yet alien. Something, some vital spark, was missing and she did not know whether the fault was hers or Brian's. Perhaps, she reflected, she should not judge it until it was finished.

Brian gave a grunt of annoyance. 'This isn't going too well,' he told her. 'But I just want to get the line of your hair exactly right. Five minutes?'

'Five minutes.'

It was not long to wait, but Dani smelt the linseed oil and turpentine that lingered in the small, light room and sighed inwardly. She would be late for Marina's dinner party if she didn't hurry. It had been a last minute invitation to make up the numbers, and Dani did not know who the other guests were, but from the tone of Marina's voice—flustered and excited—at least one of them was important.

The loud rap on the side door of the studio startled them both. Dani swivelled her eyes towards Brian expectantly, caught a mixture of exasperation and resignation on his face and guessed that he was torn between curiosity and yelling to whoever was outside to go away. All the village people knew better than to knock at that door while the big white notice, 'Danger: Artist at Work', was pinned to it. Brian had a loud voice and a quick temper, and if the notice was a little extravagant, at least, as he said, he gave people fair warning. Whoever was outside could not know him. The knocking came again, somehow peremptory, and Brian flung down his paintbrush with a muttered expletive.

'Someone's in a hurry,' Dani commented artlessly.

'Stay there for just one more minute.' Brian motioned to her to remain still. With a grunt of annoyance, he wiped his hands on a piece of rag and threw it on to the table. The knocking came yet again. 'Who the devil *is* that?'

From her chair on the low dais, Dani could not see the visitor, but from the tone of Brian's voice as he opened the door, he was not unknown to the artist, even if his appearance caused some surprise.

'What the hell are you doing here?' Dani heard Brian exclaim.

'Now there's a nice welcome.' Cool, assured, amused, the deep, attractive tone made Dani raise an eyebrow. 'How are you, Brian?'

'Okay.' The earlier surprise seemed to vanish into wary politeness. 'Why didn't you let me know you were coming?'

'And give you an opportunity to be out when I called?' Still that same lazy hint of laughter. The stranger had to be smiling. 'No, thanks.'

'Well . . . you'd better come in.' The invitation was made grudgingly. Dani knew that in the stranger's place she would have declined, chilled by the ungraciousness in Brian's voice. The stranger did not seem at all concerned.

'Thanks.'

Footsteps sounded on the bare wooden floor of the studio and Dani waited with curious interest for them to come within her line of vision. She could have turned her heard, of course, it would have been quite natural, but Brian had fussed so much as he set her up in this particular pose that she did not dare to move.

'What are you doing in this part of the world?' Brian was now trying for polite conversation, but the edge in his voice still betrayed some emotion that Dani could not quite identify.

'I've bought a property around here. Thought I'd look you up while I was in the area.'

'Oh yes? What've you bought?'

'The Manor.'

The Manor? Dani abandoned her pose and turned her head sharply. She had heard nothing in the village about the place being sold. Ever since the death of old Mrs Desmond, the local people had been speculating about its fate. Rumours that it had been bought by a pop star had brought the villagers' collective hearts into their mouths, but that had proved to be only unfounded gossip, and the Manor had now been empty for nearly three years.

'What the hell do you want with that place?' Brian asked, and Dani waited with interest for the reply as she stared at the stranger.

He was probably two inches shorter than Brian's six foot three, but the larger man in no way diminished him. He stood slightly apart from the artist, hands relaxed at his sides and an expression of polite interest on his face, yet Dani had an impression of coiled-spring tension in his body. Like a tawny tiger waiting to pounce on his prey. Dani smiled inwardly at her own fancifulness.

'I have plans for it.' The newcomer glanced around him before turning his full attention to the easel in the middle of the room. Then he looked at Dani.

She was immediately aware of sea-green eyes, the colour of the ocean on a stormy day. Eyes that held secrets; eyes that looked at her and asked her who she was and why she wasn't leaving now that Brian had a visitor; eyes that told her to go. One eyebrow lifted a fraction, and the way it curved made Dani think of the devil in a good temper. It also made her jaw set a little more firmly, and when he saw the tiny movement, his wide mobile mouth twitched into a smile.

'Ah . . .' Brian must have seen them staring at one another. ' . . . Dani, I'd like you meet Prentice McCulloch. Prentice, this is Danielle Robertson. Prentice, incidentally . . .' Brian grinned, but the smile did not quite reach his eyes, '. . . is my half-brother.'

'Miss Robertson.' Prentice nodded casually and Dani opened her mouth to correct him and then shut it again. She could be Miss Robertson as far as he was concerned. No need to draw attention to herself by explaining that her correct title should be Mrs Robertson. She contented herself with a tentative smile, but already he was looking away from her, back towards Brian.

'You aren't expecting to stay here, are you?' The thought had obviously only just occurred to the artist, and he blurted out the question impulsively. It was horribly ungracious, even for him, and as Dani watched in fascination, she saw a tinge of red appear in the portion of his cheeks not covered by the beard. So Brian Smith could blush! Dani was amused. The painter obviously realised how inhospitable his question had been and sought to retrieve the situation. 'What I mean is,' he hurried on, 'I only have one bed. If you'd told me you were coming . . .' He stopped and shrugged.

'I'm staying in Ipswich, thanks.'

'Oh. I see. Well, what do you want with the Manor?'

'In its present condition, not much.' Prentice took out a slim, gold cigarette case and offered it to his half-brother, who refused with an impatient shake of his head. 'I have to have it renovated first. It's in one hell of a state.'

The cigarettes had not been offered to Dani. She sensed that she had been mentally pigeonholed in this man's mind as simply the girl who was modelling for Brian, and therefore not worthy of attention. The thought angered her. She would have liked to have shown her displeasure by stalking out and leaving both men in their state of armed wariness, but she was also curious. What would this man do with the Manor? Live in it with his wife and children?

'It'll be an expensive project,' Brian said shrewdly. 'Business must be better than I thought. What on earth do you want with a place like that?' A thought seemed to strike him. 'Are you finally going to take the plunge and get married?'

So he wasn't married.

'No.' Prentice seemed to have abandoned any attempt to be friendly. His voice was curt and cold. 'I am not getting married. I like my life too much the way it is.' Again his eyes flicked to Dani and she guessed he was wondering if she was Brian's girl-friend. Then they slid away from her and looked at a painting leaning against the wall. Dani followed the direction of his gaze and saw that he was looking at the picture of a nude which lay, half finished and temporarily abandoned, facing into the room. His eyes returned to Dani.

The inference was obvious. The face of the nude had only been lightly sketched in with charcoal and it could be anyone. Clearly he believed that it was her and she saw his expression become contemplative, as if he was assessing her. Dani returned the stare impassively, but for a moment she was aware of tension crackling between them.

'Actually,' Prentice said, turning from her, 'I'm just on my way to a dinner party at Alder House. Do you know it?'

Dani's eyes narrowed speculatively. Alder House was the home of her sister and brother-in-law, Harry Coles. Prentice McCulloch had to be the important dinner guest. She felt her heart sink.

'Yes,' Brian nodded. 'It's only round the corner from here' His voice became openly curious. 'You know the Coles?'

'Not exactly. I'm looking around for building contractors. Harry Coles seems damn anxious to get the job . . . hence the invitation. Having a local man might have its advantages, but if the man runs his business the way he talks, he'll be working on the Manor for ever. I don't have the time for that.'

Poor Harry! Dani knew that her Suffolk-born brother-in-law did tend to measure his words before he spoke, and that he was not a gifted conversationalist, yet she resented the implied arrogance in Prentice McCulloch's words.

'Just because we live in a village, you don't have to believe we're all brainless country bumpkins!' The words were out before she could stop them.

Immediately, she became the focus of two stares; one curious and the other cold as one of Prentice's eyebrows lifted.

'I wasn't aware that I'd said you were.' The cool tones were very precise. 'I simply implied that it might be quicker to get a contractor from Ipswich . . .'

'Because Harry Coles is a craftsman who might do the job too slowly for you . . .'

'. . . and because his quotes might be too high.'

Dani bit her lip and tried to stop the red from creeping into her cheeks. Now she saw her interruption as presumptuous, and from the way he was looking at her, Prentice McCulloch agreed.

'I have to go,' she said awkwardly, wanting to be out of his sight. He was making her feel suddenly like one of her own small pupils.

'If you're working, Brian, then of course I'll leave you in peace.' There was nothing in Prentice's voice but steady politeness as he glanced at his half-brother. 'I'd hate to waste your valuable time. Or yours, Miss Robertson.' He did not look at Dani.

'It doesn't matter.' Impatiently Brian waved his hand. 'Dani can come over any time. You want a drink?'

'No, thanks.'

Dani guessed that there would never be another occasion on which Brian could ask a question like that. Prentice had been so clearly made to feel unwelcome that she sensed he would never risk a second rebuff. She watched the man's chin lift slightly in self-defensive pride and wondered again why Brian had been so rude.

'Hey, look . . .' The artist was an observant man. He must have seen the gesture, too. '. . . I'm like a bear with a sore head when I'm working. Stay and have that drink. Dani and I have finished, really we have.'

She was surprised by the suddenly conciliatory note in Brian's voice. It did not fit the man she knew, but it was the closest thing to an apology that she had ever heard the big man utter.

'Well—all right.' Prentice sounded reluctant.

'Good. Good.' Brian rubbed his hands together and his voice sounded rather too loud in the quietness of the studio. Having made his gesture of appeasement, he now seemed to be in a good mood. 'Come and tell me what you think of this.'

The two men studied the portrait of Dani as she sat uncomfortably on her chair and waited.

'Not bad,' Prentice said at last. 'She's very unusual.'

Unusual? What did he mean by that? Dani glared and Brian laughed and Prentice surveyed her with his jade eyes. Jade? They had been the colour of the sea the last time she had looked into them. Indignantly she prepared a haughty answer, annoyed by the fact that she was being treated like an inanimate object, but Prentice had moved on to something else.

'Not the only thing you're doing, I see.' He nodded towards the nude and the sunlight coming weakly through the window glinted on his hair and emphasised the auburn tints in it, making it glow like a bold autumn sunset.

'It isn't right,' Brian said despondently. 'I've spent hours over the damn thing. Maybe I should stick to landscapes.'

Dani hardly heard him. She was watching the appreciative look on Prentice McCulloch's face, and the way his eyes were moving from the picture to her and then back again. She did not need to look at the painting to remind herself of the relaxed pose of the woman, the gentle curve of her breasts, the way Brian had been clever enough to capture the healthy glow of creamy skin, she had seen it too many times before. And it wasn't her! She wanted to shout the words to the man studying it, but an inner voice told her that he would not believe her.

'I must go,' she said again, and she could feel her blush heating her cheeks. 'I'll see you later, Mr McCulloch.'

'You will?' Again that infuriating lift of his eyebrow as he stared at her through the smoke of his cigarette.

'Yes. Harry Coles is my brother-in-law.'

It was her ace and she played it triumphantly, determined to try to embarrass him as he had embarrassed her.

'Is he now?' Prentice McCulloch's expression never wavered by a fraction. His face was, Dani thought angrily, like a graven mask. What would it take to put some emotion into the bleak eyes?

'Yes.' She stood up, stretched, and deliberately turned her back on the portrait of the nude woman. 'See you, Brian.'

She turned and left the studio, running lightly up the wooden staircase outside the building that led to her own flat, above Brian's, and feeling her chagrin mount with every step she took. It was not like her to jump as precipitously into a conversation as she had. Neither was it like her to speak so sharply to a complete stranger. No wonder Brian had looked surprised.

She ran through her living room, with its cream-coloured walls and oak beams and into her bedroom, pulling her dress off quickly and changing with anxious speed. She wanted to get to Marina's house before Prentice McCulloch did. She felt somehow that it would give her an advantage to be able to greet him when he arrived rather than being late and flustered herself.

Originally her home had been part of an old barn. Brian had bought it, renovated it carefully in keeping with the neighbouring buildings, adding a studio and creating the first-floor flat. Dani had moved in as soon as it was ready and had been living there for two years.

She liked her home. She liked the wood floors that were liberally sprinkled with mats, the paintings that she had cajoled from Brian, and her huge rubber tree with its big, glossy leaves. One window in the living room looked out over the village square, and she was never lonely with the heart of the village so close to her. Gold velvet curtains framed the casement and the colour was echoed in the cushions that were scattered on the couch and the one easy chair that Dani possessed, while one wall of the room was almost completely hidden by row upon row of books.

As she changed, Dani began to remember snippets of conversations with Brian over the last year. Yes, he *had* mentioned a half-brother. It had been around the time when his parents had died, and she furrowed her forehead as she tried to remember the details. Mutual mother but different fathers. She was sure she remembered Brian saying, with a rather twisted smile, that their mother had left Prentice's father when Prentice was about two years old, and had gone to live with the man who became Brian's father.

Was that right? Dani pushed her feet into high-heeled court shoes and reached for her hairbrush. Hadn't Brian said something about being born before his parents could marry? Hadn't he said it lightly and casually, but hadn't she noticed the way his hands had twisted a piece of Mexican pottery around as he had spoken? She could also just recall the feeling she had gained at the time that Brian had not liked his half-brother, although he had admitted feeling sorry for him because he had been brought up solely by his father and hadn't met his mother again until he was adult.

Dani stepped out on to the small wood-railed balcony at the top of her stairs feeling rushed and unready for the evening ahead. Then voices floated up to her from the front door of Brian's ground-floor flat.

' . . . come and see me again. You'll be spending a fair bit of time here, I suppose.' Brian's tone was far more cordial than it had been earlier.

'Yes, I will.' The quieter assurance of Prentice. 'I want to get things started as soon as possible. I could be working on the plans this evening if I didn't have this damn dinner to go to.' There was a pause and Dani, right foot frozen on the first step of the staircase, suddenly realised that she was eavesdropping. 'What are these people like?' Prentice continued.

'The Coles? They're nice.'

'And this Dani Robertson?'

'She's a teacher at the local school.'

'Oh God, a schoolmarm! That's all I need!' It was said

in a tone of bored resignation, as if Prentice McCulloch could see a long and difficult evening ahead.

'You run along and enjoy yourself.'

Dani gritted her teeth at the laughter in Brian's voice, and the memory of what Prentice had said. A schoolmarm! How dare he! He made her sound about fifty. There was nothing wrong, she told herself indignantly, about being a school teacher. Nothing at all.

She could not walk down her stairs without them seeing and hearing her. On impulse she slipped back into her flat and watched from the window until she saw a big, blue Volvo slide away in the direction of Alder House.

Damn him! She could still hear the condescension in his voice. In just a few minutes he had succeeded in shaking her out of her usual calm, placid mood and reducing her to a furious state of agitation.

Now, as she trod carefully down her stairs, aware that they were a little precarious, she remembered another aspect of that year-old conversation with Brian. She had suggested that maybe the father of this half-brother—she hadn't known Prentice's name then—and Brian's mother had married too young. Brian had looked at her with rare compassion in his eyes and had asked her if that was what had happened to her. She had said yes. Just yes, nothing more, but he had been intuitive enough to steer the conversation into another channel.

Dani walked swiftly across the square in the wake of the Volvo that had disappeared from sight along Church Street, and cursed silently. Prentice McCulloch was dredging up memories that she would rather forget. She disliked his calm assurance and she hated even more the way he had looked at the nude portrait and then at her, raking her with his eyes before dismissing her casually.

She squared her shoulders and smiled grimly as she approached Alder House. Perhaps she would give him a few surprises during the evening.

Oh, come on, she told herself, somewhat amazed by her own militancy. What does it matter? Just get through the evening, get home and forget him. The trouble was that she suspected Prentice McCulloch would not be easy to forget.

CHAPTER TWO

'So when do you hope to move into the Manor?'

The question was asked during a lull in the conversation around the dinner table, and while Marina looked expectantly at her guest, Dani cut a neat square of the beef she was eating and wondered if her sister would get a straight answer.

The atmosphere at the dinner party was constrained. Everyone seemed to be polite but wary and they had been talking about every topic under the sun, trying to keep away from village matters in deference to their guest. However, Dani had known that the question, or one like it, would be asked at some stage. Now she glanced quickly to her right and saw Prentice McCulloch break the bread roll on his sideplate with thin, strong brown fingers before raising his eyes to meet those of his hostess.

'Hasn't Harry told you?' As Dani listened, his voice conveyed a little surprise that she was sure was feigned. 'I shan't be living there, except maybe for just a few months. I'm turning the Manor into a Country Club.'

The temperature in the room seemed to drop, almost as if someone had lifted the roof and the ceilings off the house and exposed them all to the chill evening air. Marina stared, first at Prentice and then at her husband, and Bill and Elsie Chamberlain, the other guests at the table, exchanged one quick glance before bending their heads to their food again.

Dani saw all this in one swift, encompassing glance, and

then turned her own eyes to Harry. He looked uncomfortable as he smiled half-heartedly and he pulled a wry face in Dani's direction as she shook her head slightly in exasperation.

'Harry?' Marina's voice both accused and asked for an explanation. 'Why didn't you tell me?'

'Not your business, my dear. Mr McCulloch can do what he pleases with his property.'

'What exactly do you mean by a country club?' Marina turned her head back to look at her guest. 'Licensed premises? An hotel? What sort of thing are you planning?'

'Initially something on quite a small scale,' Prentice said smoothly. 'Good food, a few bedrooms, bars . . .'

'So it's really an hotel.'

'A kind of hotel,' he agreed, and if he was aware of any antagonism from his fellow diners, he ignored it. 'But later on I hope to add a swimming pool and a sauna and a jacuzzi. The whole place will be open to non-residents, of course, and with the acreage around the Manor, I hope to put in a nine-hole golf course and tennis courts.'

'Good lord!' Bill took a hasty sip of his wine and Dani knew what he was thinking. His beautiful Suffolk-pink cottage backed on to the Manor grounds. No doubt he was wondering what sporting facility was going to be the closest to his carefully tended garden. Golf balls among his peas, tennis balls with the roses, or the shouts of people enjoying a swim and destroying his peace?

'Mr McCulloch, this is a quiet village.' Elsie was the first to muster some form of coherent statement. 'And I must say, I'm not looking forward to the idea of having an hotel right on our front doorsteps. People coming and going . . .'

'A country club,' Prentice corrected her smoothly. 'And

I do assure you, Mrs Chamberlain, that there will be no rowdy behaviour.'

They had begun the dinner by tentatively calling one another by their Christian names. Now it seemed that war had been declared. Dani watched Prentice covertly from her place next to him. Completely composed, his self-assurance wrapped around him like a cloak, this bringer of bad news sat quietly in his chair while his fingers played idly with his bread roll. Dani watched the tell-tale fingers and knew, suddenly, that the confidence was partially a pose, and that the man was not as relaxed as he appeared to be. The bread roll was disintegrating into a small pile of white and brown flakes, resembling a miniature snowstorm.

'Well, I'm sure everything will be fine,' Harry said heartily. 'We mustn't judge before we know.'

All eyes turned to him. Prentice smiled slightly, but the eyes of all the others accused him of siding with the enemy. Harry, Dani realised, could not be considered impartial. He was prepared to carry out the work that would turn the Manor from a shabby—yes, Dani had to admit that it was shabby—house, loved and known by all the villagers, into a smart hotel.

She had been very quiet all the evening, earning herself an annoyed stare from Marina for not contributing enough to the conversation. Now she felt she should enter into the discussion.

'I think it'll be a terrible thing for the village,' she said clearly, and Marina's eyes opened wide in surprise. Dani looked directly at Prentice McCulloch and the icy emerald green of his eyes looked back at her.

'Why?' he asked quietly. 'What's so terrible?'

She was ready for that question. 'We're a small community,' she informed him, 'just as Elsie said. The Manor is partly within the bounds of the village. It's going to affect all of us. The noise—cars coming and going— maybe music late in the evening. This is a peaceful parish . . .'

'Parochial.' He nodded. 'Just the word I'd have used.'

Somehow he made the word sound like an insult. Dani laid down her knife and fork and nodded.

'I'm sure you would,' she agreed pleasantly. 'We aren't exactly living in the dark ages here, but it's true that big changes tend to affect everyone.'

'You think it's a bad thing for an hotel to create jobs in the village?'

'Not necessarily, but . . .'

'Do you think your local shopkeepers will object to the extra trade?'

'If there is any.'

'There will be.' He turned in his seat so that he was facing her directly. 'What you're saying,' he continued implacably, 'is that this village doesn't want change. Not change of any kind. Are you speaking for everyone or just for yourself?'

'I think we're all concerned,' Bill Chamberlain said. 'My own cottage is next to the grounds . . .'

'I know, Mr Chamberlain.' Just as swiftly Prentice turned his attention to the older man. 'Believe me, there will be no facilities for swimming or golf anywhere near your house or anyone else's.'

'The Manor is very old.' Dani retreated to her second line of attack. 'If you're going to turn it into a . . . country club . . . I assume that you'll be altering the existing structure quite a bit.'

'Naturally.' Again she was subjected to a cool scrutiny.

'Then you'll be spoiling a very beautiful house.' Dani had a momentary feeling that she had won a victory. 'It would be criminal to change it around.' There was a sudden ominous silence. Dani watched Prentice's face and saw it harden into a mask of granite. 'It should be preserved,' she continued defiantly, 'not turned into some kind of money-making machine for . . .'

The gleaming jade eyes and the lips that suddenly thinned into a hard line warned her that she had gone too far.

'Come and help me, Dani.' Marina's voice made the request into an order. Dumbly, a scarlet tide of embarrassment staining her face, Dani left her seat and followed her sister into the kitchen.

'What are you trying to do?' Marina hissed as soon as the door was closed behind them. 'God knows, the man isn't exactly the world's best guest, but for heaven's sake don't antagonise him any more!'

'Do you want an hotel right on your doorstep?' Dani challenged her sister in a hushed whisper that did not hide her anger.

'No,' Marina admitted, 'I don't. Not really. On the other hand, the man is right. If Harry gets the contract to do the renovations, then he'll keep his men in work for quite a while.' She held up her hand as Dani exclaimed. 'All right, so that's selfish. Maybe it is. But how many youngsters around here can you think of who can't get a job? I can think of seven or eight without trying. The man's right. This hotel, country club, whatever you want to call it, will create jobs.'

'And ruin a beautiful old house,' Dani snapped back. 'Or doesn't that matter?'

'Of course it matters!' Marina began to arrange coffee

cups on a tray. 'But the man has bought the place. We can't stop him.'

Dani suspected that her sister was right. She was also honest enough to question her own motives. Perhaps she would not have spoken so strongly had it not been for the casual arrogance of the man. She felt her anger rise again.

'Hey,' Marina's voice softened. 'Take that light of battle out of your eye. Heavens, I haven't seen you so angry for years!'

'He's treating us like village idiots!' Dani whispered furiously. 'I've never seen such an infuriating . . .' She stopped. Marina was regarding her with her head tilted on one side. 'What are you staring at?' Dani asked crossly.

'I think you're over-reacting,' her sister said, and she grinned suddenly. 'He's very attractive, isn't he?'

'That has nothing to do with it!'

'No? All right.' Marina checked the percolator and put the dessert dishes into Dani's hands. 'Now just you calm down,' she said severely. 'The man is my guest and I'd like you to be civil to him.'

'Civil?'

'That's what I said.'

Back in the dining room there was an atmosphere of cool politeness. Dani slid into her seat and kept her head down, guiltily aware that she was partially the cause of the constraint and not daring to look in Prentice McCulloch's direction. The headiness of her anger had vanished and she felt stupid, like a schoolgirl who had been reprimanded by her teacher. She longed to escape.

Then she became aware, not for the first time that evening, that her right shoe was pinching her slightly, and she wriggled her foot to try to ease the discomfort. She felt the high heel descend upon something that was not carpet, and the man by her side stiffened.

Oh no. Dani knew immediately what she had done. She had put the heel of her shoe down on to his foot and he would never, never in a million years, believe that it was an accident. She waited for the storm, head bent and with a terrible feeling of panic rising in her, but when he did not instantly exclaim with pain, she found the courage to look at him.

He was talking to Elsie Chamberlain across the table, and not by word or tone or movement did he indicate that anything unusual had happened. He did not even look at her. Dani relaxed slightly, grudgingly grateful to him for not compounding the trouble that she was in already, and after a few more seconds she found the courage to talk to Harry about a London show that they had both seen recently.

When she first felt a knee nudging hers, she thought it was an accident and moved her leg away slightly. The persistent knee followed, moving gently against her own in a subtle but insistent pressure. Outraged, Dani turned her head to glare at Prentice McCulloch, but he was still talking, not looking at her, and any form of verbal protest died away in her throat before it could be uttered.

How dare he! The knee moved again and Dani shifted her leg as far away as she could, furious that such a small action could make her feel so nervous. It was difficult to equate Prentice's calm, businesslike manner with the knee that had rubbed so suggestively against her own.

The dinner party was not a success. Dani was unsurprised when Prentice got up to leave after the coffee had been served, declining a brandy on the grounds that he was driving. Then he looked at Dani.

'May I offer you a lift home?' He faced her and smiled, and Dani's heart seemed to lurch into her throat.

That smile changed his whole face; lightening it, transforming it, giving it a vitality that up until then had been missing. Dani found herself returning it simply because it was so warm and so irresistible. For an instant she would have sworn that there was no one but herself and Prentice in the room.

'Thank you.' She accepted his invitation gravely and then wondered why. Surely she was not so young and so naïve that she could be swayed by one smile?

She was still wondering why she had acquiesced as he closed the passenger door of the Volvo for her and then went around the car and slid behind the steering wheel, the width of the car making a safe gap between them.

Safe? Dani wondered why the word had crossed her mind. Of course she was safe! He could hardly pounce on her while he was driving, and he could not get lost between Alder House and her home. Neither did he look like the kind of man to indulge in an unprofitable wrestling match in the front seats. Dani smiled at the picture the thought invoked.

'Something funny?' He started the engine and waved to his host and hostess before setting the car into gear, releasing the handbrake and moving away.

'No.' A minute later she was frowning as the car turned right, away from her flat.

'You're going the wrong way,' she said.

'No I'm not. I'm taking you to see the Manor.' He did not look at her, but she had an impression of anger simmering below a veneer of calmness.

'Why?' She refused to protest.

'Because I want to show it to you.'

'I've seen it before. And it's dark.'

'So I'll put the lights on.'

'All right.' She would not give him the satisfaction of asking more questions. She knew it would probably please him to know that her curiosity was aroused.

Dani sat quietly by Prentice's side while they negotiated the long drive of the Manor, and preceded him silently into the blackness of the big hall, standing quite still while he moved around in the dark looking for the lights. When he found them and the hall was illuminated, she blinked and stared around her. She had not been in the house since the death of Mrs Desmond.

'Look at this staircase!' She walked over to it and ran her hand lovingly over the smooth wood of the newel, following the line of the banister upwards. 'It's beautiful.'

'Yes, it is.' A white handkerchief was passed to her. 'It's also dirty.'

He was right. The dust lay thickly on the wood, and she scrubbed at her palm abstractedly as she followed him into the biggest of the reception rooms, her eye immediately going to the fireplace that was the focal point.

'Come and look at this.' He led the way across to the windows and she followed him obediently, high heels echoing hollowly in the emptiness of the room. He pushed at the window frame. 'Dry rot,' he said succinctly. 'Some of these will have to be replaced.'

'Some renovation is bound to be necessary,' she pointed out reasonably.

'Work out how many windows there are in the house. They'll all have to have attention some time soon.'

'You didn't have to buy it,' she reminded him quietly.

'No.' He did not seem prepared to say any more, and

she walked over to the fireplace and stared down into the grate.

'What will this room be?' she asked. 'One of the bars?'

'Possibly.'

'Hmm.' She was still smarting over the knee-rubbing incident and the fact that he had assumed that she was willing to be brought to the Manor late at night. 'I can see it all now.' She glanced around the room, carefully avoiding looking at Prentice who stood in the centre of it. 'You could call it "the Hawaiian bar". Pictures of Maui and Oahu on the walls, fairy lights and plastic pineapples . . .'

Why was she provoking him so badly? She heard the hiss of his indrawn breath although she was several yards from him.

'Don't be such a fool!' His voice cut across the space between them like the lash of a whip. 'What do you think I am?'

'I don't know,' she retorted. 'The Manor has always been someone's home. I hate the idea of it being turned into some fancy place with saunas and . . .' She could not think of anything bad enough.

'Come with me.' He turned and stalked, straight-backed from the room, and she pulled a face at his retreating figure and wandered after him, saddened by the dingy delapidation of the place. It had always looked a little shabby in Mrs Desmond's day, had always given an air of being slightly frayed at the edges, but now that the house was empty, the faded wallpapers and the scuffed woodwork made the place look neglected and without dignity.

Dani followed Prentice up the stairs, stopping at the top to peer at a group of tiny holes in one part of the banister that he indicated with a silent, pointing forefinger, and then wandered behind him along the dark, dusty corridors to the back of the house. Here it seemed that the decay was even more advanced, and she wrinkled her nose at the musty smell.

Prentice opened a door, reached in to switch on the light, and the naked bulb illuminated a small, bare room. Dani stared.

'What am I supposed to see?' she asked. She walked past him as he leaned against the doorframe, intending to step into the room to see what she was missing. He caught hold of her arm, and his grip was fierce.

'I shouldn't actually go in there,' he said mildly. 'Not unless you'd like a quick trip to the kitchen.'

'What?'

'The floor,' he said patiently, 'wouldn't stand your weight.'

'Oh no!'

'Oh yes.' They were wedged together in the doorway and his hand was still tight on her arm. 'I've got two other rooms in the same state. The Desmonds locked them up and, I would imagine, forgot about them.'

'Mrs Desmond didn't even go upstairs for the last year she was alive,' Dani remembered.

'I've also got wet rot, damp, unsafe chimneys, roof timbers to replace and a few minor details to attend to like bringing a Victorian kitchen up to date.'

'So why *did* you buy it?' Dani tried to wriggle her arm free, but he seemed reluctant to release her.

'Because I liked it and it suited my purpose.' Finally he released her. 'I shall renovate where I can, and what can't be saved . . .' He let the sentence tail away into silence.

'I didn't know it was so bad,' Dani said softly, almost to herself.

'It doesn't take long for a place like this to deteriorate.'

'But the Desmonds loved it so much! They'd been here for generations.'

'I know.' Prentice closed the door and locked it. 'But they didn't have the money to keep it going. Not in recent years, anyway.'

Dani turned away from him, depressed by what she had seen. Yet she was still not reassured of the Manor's ultimate fate. This man could do anything he liked; totally obliterate all the character in the house in his determination to make his investment pay.

'I'm going to hate it,' she said quietly.

'You'd rather see the place fall down?'

'Of course not.' She began to walk back along the corridor, tossing the words to him over her shoulder. 'It's just that the Manor was always such a part of village life.'

'It still can be.' His footsteps drew nearer so that he was close behind her. 'When I get the golf course laid out, I hope the village people will want to use it. I hope you'll use it.'

'I don't play golf.'

'What is the matter with you?' Once again he caught hold of her arm and pulled her to an abrupt halt. She swung around to face him, and the dimness of the passage shadowed his face intriguingly, making him seem mysterious and remote. 'I expect to find that some of the older people in the village might resent the changes,' he continued flatly. 'But surely you have the intelligence to see that a country club could be an asset here. Or are you too damn insular?'

The tension crackled between them like static electricity. Dani knew that her own arguments were weak, fostered more by the love of a nice old house than by practical reasons, but their differences were more than just the sum of two people seeing something from different sides. It had become a more personal clash, his will against hers, and Dani did not understand her own emotions. She felt anger; anger that was not so much directed against what he was doing as against the man himself. She felt threatened by him, overpowered by him, and her wish to fight him seemed to come from some part of Dani Robertson that she had never known before.

'Please let go of my arm,' she said steadily and with as much dignity as she could dredge up from her shaken emotions. 'You really don't have to manhandle me . . .' There, she was doing it again! Trying to needle him into a further sharp exchange of words. What was wrong with her?

'You'd rather have walked into that room?' he asked. 'Next time, I'll let you.'

'There won't be a next time.'

'Good.'

There were some people, Dani thought philosophically as she walked away from him, who just did not get along with other people. She and Prentice McCulloch were obviously two of them. She would avoid him in the future.

They walked down the stairs to the hall in a thick and tingling silence. Dani was aware of him with every step that she took, and the back of her neck prickled suddenly as she realised that she had taken a risk in coming to the house at all. She did not know him and yet she had calmly allowed him to bring her here and to show her around the empty rooms without a thought in her head that it could be dangerous. She must be crazy!

'Will you take me home now?' she asked, and she was

proud that her voice did not wobble with her sudden
misgivings. 'Or would you prefer me to walk?'

'I wouldn't dream of letting you walk.' His voice was a
silken purr of politeness. 'Just come and take a look at the
kitchens before you go.'

Not waiting for her refusal, he turned and strode
through another door at the back of the hall and, reluctantly, Dani trudged after him. In the kitchen she glanced
around her without much interest, and shivered as the
chill of the room hit her.

'I've been here before,' she said. 'It isn't wonderful, I
know that, but I've seen worse.' Casually she crossed her
arms around herself and wandered over to stare into the
old, deep sink under the window. A fat, black, long-legged
spider stared malevolently back.

Dani could not help the shiver of distaste that trembled
through her, nor could she stop taking an instinctive step
backwards as if the spider was going to come out of its
resting place and crawl over her. The flagstones were
uneven, and she caught her heel in one of the gaps,
pitching sideways with a gasp of alarm.

'Too much wine?' His arms caught and held her and,
for a moment, while she recovered her balance, she felt his
lean, hard body taking her weight. What would it be like
to . . .

Confused by a half-formed thought that Prentice
McCulloch's arms had a strength that she had not suspected, and that she felt suddenly safe within them, she
struggled to be free.

'No,' she said crossly. 'I have not had too much wine.
There's a spider . . .'

'Oh?' Interested, he peered into the cracked sink. 'He's
a big one,' he acknowledged. 'But he won't hurt you.'

'I know he won't hurt me!' Dani retorted. 'I just don't like them. I never have.' And if he was sadistic enough to pick it up and threaten her with it, she was sufficiently unnerved to have hysterics.

'Come back and see this place when it's finished.' He spared the spider one more glance and turned to her. 'Will you do that?'

'I don't think so.' Her heart was still pounding from that brief, disturbing closeness between them. 'I prefer to remember it the way it was when Mrs Desmond was alive.' And yet she also knew she would not be able to forget the forlorn emptiness of the house that she had sensed this evening.

'Judged and found guilty already.' White lines of temper appeared suddenly at each side of his nose. 'All right, Miss Robertson, that's fine with me. I can live without your narrow-minded prejudice.'

'Prejudice?'

'That's what I said.' He banged his hand suddenly against the wooden drainer next to the sink and Dani jumped. She prayed that it would not disturb the spider. 'I can live without your approval,' he continued frostily. 'I was simply trying to be reasonable, but that doesn't appear to be a word you've ever heard of.'

'Maybe I just don't like get-rich-quick schemes . . .' Her words died away as she saw, out of the corner of her eye, his hand moving on the drainer. For one terrible moment she thought he was going to hit her and took a half step backwards to avoid the blow, but as she watched in fascination, the fingers curled themselves into a fist until the knuckles shone bone-white, and she sensed he was battling with himself to keep his temper. It was an awesome display of controlled power and Dani—knowing from her own experience the strength in those fingers—shivered a little and blamed the coldness of the room as she watched the fist tremble with the force being exerted. Then, suddenly, his fingers relaxed and stretched.

'I'll take you home now,' he said, and his voice was completely calm. 'Where do you live?'

'Above Brian.' She walked out of the kitchen ahead of him and made her way outside with yet another long, cold silence between them.

'Do you often pose for him?' The question was asked as the car slid slowly down the drive to the road.

Dani wanted to laugh. She could guess what he was thinking.

'Sometimes,' she admitted evenly. Let him think what he liked. He had accused her of being prejudiced and insular. Perhaps this would confuse his opinion. Not that she cared what he thought anyway.

'Put your seat belt on, please.' The same request had been made as they left Alder House, and Dani complied.

'I do know the law, you know.' She could not resist the tart comment.

'Good.' He seemed intent on his driving.

'I'm sorry I stood on your foot,' she said impulsively, nearly as unnerved by the quietness in the car as she had been by his controlled display of temper. 'It was an accident.'

'I'm sorry I knocked your knee,' he replied smoothly. 'That was an accident, too.'

So he didn't believe her, as she did not believe him. Sighing to herself Dani stared out of the side window, acknowledging that he was entitled to his doubts. One more minute and she would be free. She counted the seconds off in her mind, and had unbuckled the seat belt and opened the door almost before the car had stopped.

'Thank you for the lift,' she said politely. 'And thank you for the—guided tour.'

'My pleasure.' The formalities were being observed. His tone was quiet and even. 'I'll see you again some time.'

'Goodnight.'

'Goodnight, Miss Robertson.'

It had been a disturbing evening. Dani climbed the wooden stairs to her flat and unlocked the door, letting tiredness sweep over her. She felt as though she had fought some kind of battle and lost and when sleep would not come to her as she lay in her bed, she blamed Prentice McCulloch.

It was infuriating. Every time she closed her eyes, she saw him as if his face was imprinted indelibly on her brain. In her mind's eye she could recall him perfectly, as though she had been looking at him every day for a year, and she turned on to her side restlessly, trying to block out the image of his eyes, his mouth, his stubborn jaw and the long, oddly vulnerable, sweep of his throat.

What else could she think about? For once the progress of her small pupils failed to engross her as it usually did, and even her enthusiasm for a new class project waned as she tried to concentrate on it. She turned her mind into other channels and thought about a small, dark-haired baby girl whom she had never seen, but who had been described to her in a recent letter from her mother.

Jennifer Ann. Six months old, placid and beautiful. Daughter of her ex-husband and his new wife. Dani had waited to feel jealousy when she had learned of the birth of the baby, but the emotion had never occurred. All she had felt was satisfaction that Keith had finally found what he was looking for, and a curious contentment, as though the arrival of Jennifer Ann had been the seal on the ending of that part of her life.

Dani moved restlessly. They had been so young, she and Keith. Young and wilful and unable to bear being apart from one another. It had seemed such a triumph to overcome the concern and advice of both his parents and her own and get married, and such a feeling of smugness to believe that they were right and that they would spend the rest of their lives on a candyfloss cloud of love and happiness.

'Damn!' Dani turned her face into the cool cotton of her pillow and pulled the covers up closely around her ears, wincing from the teenager she had been.

Had Prentice McCulloch ever been married? Oh no, not him again! Once more Dani rolled on to her back, furious with herself for having allowed her thoughts to swing full circle. He was an attractive and fascinating man whom she had met twice. He was plainly not interested in her and she—Dani told herself crossly—was most definitely not interested in him. She gave her pillow an angry thump, closed her eyes determinedly and began to count sheep. But they all had jade-green eyes.

CHAPTER THREE

IN THE weeks that followed Prentice McCulloch's purchase of the Manor, the village talked of little else. Dani understood and sympathised. The Manor had always been a focal point of community life, just as the church and the village hall and the school were. The PTA committee were worrying about where they could hold the annual fête this year, and Dani herself had suddenly realised that the nature rambles she had enjoyed with the children in the summer months through the more remote parts of the estate would now have to be curtailed.

The weather had turned much warmer on the morning Dani heard her alarm clock ringing. She rolled over to switch it off and then allowed herself the luxury of waking up slowly, yawning and stretching and then kicking back the covers in a sudden impulsive movement as she remembered that Brian should have left for an appointment in London half an hour before and she had not been awoken by the noisy engine of his old Morris 1000 Traveller.

In her skimpy nightdress and with bare feet, she padded over to the window that looked down on the yard where they kept their cars and, rubbing her eyes, she stared sleepily downwards. One Morgan 4/4, a car that Brian was renovating in his spare time, her own Ford Fiesta, and one Morris Traveller. Brian had not gone!

'Oh!' Angry with him for having overslept, and with herself for behaving like an anxious hen with one chick, she ran back to the bedroom and began to dress. She wriggled jeans up over the briefs that clung to her slender hips and dragged a T-shirt over her head without bothering with a bra. Four impatient sweeps of her hairbush over her hair restored it to a sleek and shining cap, and then she was pulling on her running shoes as she hopped towards her door, frantic to get Brian up and on his way. Perhaps if she lent him her car he would make better time. This appointment was important to him, and from the silence under her feet, he did not even appear to have woken up.

She took the last four steps of the flight of stairs in one leap, landing neatly, and then swung around to the front door of the barn.

'Brian!' Impatiently she hammered on the door and then opened it to peer inside. 'Oh, Brian!' On his couch-cum-bed, in the dimness of the room, the artist slept on, blankets pulled up almost over his head. From the bottom of the bed, from which the covers had been dragged, one bare foot stuck out. 'Brian!' She ran across the room, her rubber-shod feet making little sound. 'Wake up, will you?' She tugged at the outline in the bed.

'What?' It was an almost inaudible mumble of sound as the sleeper pulled away from her hands, hunching further down under the covers.

'Will you get up!' She made her voice louder and shook his shoulder more impatiently. 'Come on!' And then, with a mixture of anxiety and crossness, 'Brian!'

'Oh God!'

It didn't sound quite like Brian. What she could see of his hair that was not covered by bedclothes did not appear to be the same colour, and the shape did not seem bulky enough.

'Brian?' This time she made the name a question, but as

the covers were slowly turned back and one eye stared balefully at her, she put her hand up to her mouth in an involuntary gesture of surprise and alarm. 'Oh,' she said lamely. 'Good morning.'

'Is it?' Prentice opened the other eye and glared at her. 'Do you make a habit of waking my brother up like this?'

'Of course not.' Dani took a step backwards. 'But he has an appointment in London, an important one, and he should have left half an hour ago.'

'He did.' Yawning, Prentice scrubbed his hands over his eyes and rolled over on to his back to stare at her. 'I lent him the Volvo. Thought he might stand a better chance of getting there in a decent car.' No wonder she had not heard the sound of Brian's engine coughing into life.

'Oh. I'm sorry. I didn't realise . . .' Dani was caught in the grip of unreasonable panic. This sleepy-eyed man was nothing like the Prentice McCulloch she had met those few weeks ago. Where was the confidence and the self-possession? This vulnerable stranger was catching at her heart and making her breath come more quickly.

He smiled, and she felt her pulses leap. It was too early in the morning for her to be able to cope with the wonderful sweetness of that smile.

'Don't worry,' he said. 'I know what Brian's like. Thank you for caring enough about him to be worried.'

This wasn't Prentice McCulloch! This wasn't the man she had met and been so disturbed by a few weeks before. This man, who watched her as he reclined lazily in his bed, was relaxed and very, very human. Prentice sat up suddenly and reached for her wrist.

'You don't have to run away,' he told her mildly. 'I'm

not going to eat you.' The covers slid downwards to his waist.

Oh lord! Dani wanted to escape from the jade eyes and the curving mouth that seemed to mock her, and from the tanned body revealed by the falling bedclothes. Did he sleep in the nude and was one of them about to be very embarrassed? She doubted that it would be him.

'I have to get ready for school,' she protested weakly. 'I have to change, have breakfast . . .' Getting to school early was one of the things she prided herself upon, but timing was all important.

'Oh? You aren't going to school like that?' His eyes ran down the T-shirt to the figure-hugging jeans.

'Of course not!' She laughed at the idea. 'These were the first things I could find.'

'You look like a kid.' His gaze slid upwards. 'Well, part of you does,' he amended with a lift of his eyebrows, and Dani remembered how the T-shirt clung to her body and felt the red creeping into her cheeks.

'I have to go,' she said again. 'I've got a busy day today.'

'No, not yet. Tell me what's happening in the village.' His hand was still on her wrist, not hurting her but holding her securely. 'I think you should be civil to me after you were rude enough to wake me up.'

Dani wanted to know what he was doing there anyway, but she did not like to ask. He had given her an ideal opportunity to talk to him, however, and for the sake of the village and the school she loved so much, Dani did not hesitate. She did not want to stay with the man, but this was more important than her own feelings. With a daring that she did not know she possessed, she perched on the side of his bed and looked straight at him.

'I'm on the committee for the annual fête,' she told him quietly. 'We have to decide if we can hold one this year, and if so, where.'

'Where do you usually hold it?' A glitter of understanding appeared in his eyes. 'Or could I guess?'

'Mrs Desmond always allowed us to hold it on the front lawns of the Manor,' Dani admitted. 'We always left the place immaculate . . . we're always very careful . . .'

'And there's nowhere else?'

'No. No one has a garden big enough to take all the stalls and the marquees.'

'Marquees?'

'Only little ones,' Dani told him hastily.

'I see.'

There was a short silence and Dani wondered frantically how long she would be able to keep her eyes pinned to his face when her curiosity was niggling at her to let her glance slide downwards, just a little.

Keith, when she had been married to him, had been nearly nineteen and had possessed the body of a youth. Prentice McCulloch had the body of a man; a powerful man whose conservative clothing completely camouflaged the smooth, muscular planes of his chest and arms. She wanted to look at him again, and as the thought stayed in her mind she shrank inwardly from the tiny shaft of desire that ran through her. What would it be like to touch that warm, tanned skin? What would it be like to be drawn closely against the strength of his body and to rest her head on his shoulder? What would . . .

'I don't see why you shouldn't use the grounds again this year.' What was he saying? Startled, Dani focused her eyes on his face again. 'The club won't be opening for several months.' He shrugged. 'There's no reason why you shouldn't have the use of the grounds.'

'Why . . . thank you!' She was too surprised to say much more. It was so unexpected, this generous gesture of his. 'It's very kind of you.'

'It'll delay the need for you to find another place at short notice.' He sounded offhand. 'Do you need any part of the house, too?'

'Well, the kitchens?' She knew she was perhaps asking for too much, but he seemed to be in a good mood.

'Such as they are, they're yours.' Again that casualness. 'Tell your committee they can come and go as they please. Most of the work's taking place around the back, but they can liaise with Harry about that and make sure they don't get in his way.'

'Thank you.'

'My pleasure.'

The committee would be so relieved! Dani could imagine their faces when she told them the good news, and involuntarily she smiled.

'Something funny?' He missed nothing.

'Not really. I'm just happy we've had a reprieve. The fête usually raises a lot of money for the school and for other clubs in the village, too. The over-sixties club, the youth club . . .'

'I'm sure.' He interrupted her, but he was smiling. 'Maybe I'll come along and see for myself.'

'You should open it!' Dani was carried away by her enthusiasm. 'The house is yours now, and . . .'

' . . . and maybe not.' The smile widened, quirking the corners of his mouth upwards. 'I think that might be rather too much for the village to take, don't you?'

Reluctantly Dani nodded. 'Maybe,' she admitted.

'Sorry. Oh!' Another thought struck her. 'One more thing.'

'Lady, don't you think you've wrung enough out of me for one day?'

'The children always used to have a nature ramble across the bottom of the estate,' she said breathlessly. 'Through the spinney and over the stream . . .'

' . . . and you'd like to do it again this year.' He finished the sentence for her. 'Well, why not? But I'm soon going to have the stream cleared.'

'We'll come today,' Dani promised. 'You won't even know we're around.'

'Hmm.' He seemed to doubt the veracity of that statement. 'Well, just be careful none of the kids fall in and drown. I'm unpopular enough as it is.'

The remark could have been uttered in such a way as to make the man seem uncaring, and yet Dani knew instinctively that it was not meant like that. It was as though he was somehow ashamed of the gesture he had made to her, and was covering up his generosity.

'They won't drown,' she said confidently. 'Thank you.'

'My pleasure.' He stretched his arms above his head, and this time Dani could not restrain herself from staring at him. There was such strength in that lean, supple frame. Vitality flowed out to her from the tips of his flexed fingers all the way down his arching body to his waist, and she felt herself begin to melt inside in sheer wanton need of his power.

No! She stopped herself sharply. It was stupid to think like that. Yet there was something disturbingly intimate about the unself-consciousness of his action, as though she had sat on the side of his bed many times before and his nakedness was something very familiar to her.

'I have to go.' Awkwardly she got to her feet, aware of how close they had been on Brian's couch and how she had just been staring at him openly. 'Or I really shall be late for school.'

'I'd hate to make you late.' As if a mask had been dropped into place, he became cool and polite. Only his rumpled hair and his lack of clothes were reminders of the unguarded man she had seen only seconds before.

'Yes. Well . . .' She could think of no suitable way to close the conversation. '. . . thank you once again. You've been very kind.'

'I have, haven't I?' He seemed a little surprised. 'You must have caught me on a good day. Or before I was awake.'

'Sorry.'

'So you should be.'

Dani did not realise that her watch was missing until after she had returned to school from her afternoon ramble with the infants. It was small and gold but its importance to her was not in the value. It had been a twenty-first birthday present from her parents.

Worried and apprehensive, she saw all her charges on their way home, and then began to retrace her steps, her eyes scanning the ground all the time, walking back down the street along which she had just come.

On the pavement it was possible to keep up a reasonable pace, but when she turned into the narrow road that passed the main entrance to the Manor, she stopped and bit her lip in frustration. So much ground to cover, and her first search had to be along the edge of the village pond.

It was not a nice pond. For a long time now, Dani had

been urging the parish council to have it dredged and cleaned, but so far her lobbying had fallen on deaf ears. Algae grew so thickly on it that she had thrown a small stone into the middle to demonstrate this to the children, and it had been a couple of seconds before the green crust on the pond had been sufficiently weakened to let the stone sink from sight. The children knew it well, of course, but Dani had stopped there to try and point out some of the small birds that made their homes in the trees that grew on the far side, and a couple of uncommon plants that were struggling for survival in their deep shade.

If she had lost it around here, then she would probably never find it. Dani hunted along the edge of the pond and then promised herself that she would look again on her way home. The smell of rotting vegetation made her wrinkle her nose in disgust, and once again she wondered how the village could stand having such an eyesore.

Abandoning the search there for a while, she climbed the stile that led into the field she had so recently crossed with the children, staring around her in dismay at the acres of grass before her. It had seemed quite a small field when she had last walked over it, but now it only served to underline the enormity of her task.

The sun beat down strongly on her back and penetrated the thin cotton of her blouse to heat her shoulders. She sat on the top of the stile and scanned the grass for a few minutes, looking for a reflection of the sun's rays off her watch glass, but she could see nothing. With an inward shrug at her own optimism, she climbed down and set off across the field, her eyes raking the greenness around her, and just occasionally raising her head to look at her destination so that she did not completely lose track of where she was going.

It was more pleasant to search around in the spinney, when she finally reached it, because the leaves protected her from the direct glare of the sun. Yet it was also more difficult because it was hard for her to keep track of every single tree and shrub. She just could not be sure that she had not missed some vital piece of ground.

Eventually she reached the shallow, slow-moving stream that wound its way sluggishly around stones and over weed. Prentice was right to want to have it cleared, she thought. It was not pretty in its present state, although a haven for tiny creatures that would be disturbed when it was invaded by men with spades and rakes.

Dani could remember exactly where they had crossed the stream, and she sat down on the bank and let her eyes work for her, scanning every centimetre of grass and stones and mud, and then peering into the water. It was hopeless! She kept her eyes on the stream, unwilling to give up the search even for a moment, but she allowed her shoulders to droop and she rested her elbows on her bent knees and let her chin drop into her hand.

'What are you doing?' The soft voice made her jump and she tilted her head back to see Prentice McCulloch a little further up on the other side of the stream, his hands in the pockets of his trousers as he watched her.

'I've lost my watch,' she said simply. 'I'm just sitting here looking for a minute before I go back through the spinney. How did you know I was here?'

'Saw you from one of the bedroom windows. I thought you seemed to be looking for something. Can I help?'

'Oh.' Suddenly the tears were close, and she blinked them away furiously, knowing that it was the quiet concern in his voice that had caused them.

'You'd rather I went away again?' The green eyes were quizzical and she smiled wanly.

'No, of course not. It was nice of you to come, but . . .' she gestured around her hopelessly, ' . . . it could be anywhere.' A great lump rose in her throat at the thought of never having her watch on her wrist again. She had loved it so much.

'We'll find it.' He crossed the stream as he spoke, his long legs spanning its width easily, and when he held out his hand to her, she took it gratefully and allowed him to pull her to her feet. 'It's too early to give up yet,' he continued, and in the quietness of the spinney his voice sounded gentle. 'Where have you looked?'

'Everywhere.'

'If you'd looked everywhere, you'd have found it.' He squeezed her fingers and she felt her heart contract with the pressure. He was trying to help, he almost seemed concerned for her, and she smiled. The least she could do was to allow him to raise her hopes a little.

'That's right,' she agreed. 'And I'm sure it's on this side of the stream. I was lifting the children across.'

'So you could have dropped it in the water?'

'I suppose so.'

'I see.' As she watched him, his eyes scanned the narrow stretch of water and then returned to the same stone she had stood upon to lift the children across. 'Did that take your weight without sinking?' He nodded to the stone without looking at her.

'Yes.'

'Well, I'm not sure that it'll bear mine, so just in case . . .'

He had a tweed sports jacket slung over his shoulder. As she waited, he threw it to the ground and rolled up the sleeves of his immaculate cream shirt. Then he took off his socks and shoes and placed them neatly side by side, obviously not at all confident of the stability or the safety of the rock. And he was right. As he stepped on to it, it sank just enough to allow a trickle of water to flow over it, and he flashed Dani a grin of triumph that his judgement had been so accurate before crouching down so that he could run his hands along the bed of the stream.

The water was not deep, but Dani could imagine the squelchy mud and weeds at the bottom and she wrinkled her nose, hating the idea of sinking her own hands into the silted bed. If her watch was really in there, then it was probably ruined.

The sun glinted on his head, highlighting the auburn tints, and she leaned against a tree and watched him, fascinated by his absorption, her eyes running along the curved line of his spine to the back of his unprotected neck upon which the sun shone hotly.

'You'll never find it.' She felt that she had to make him give up his task. He was a stranger, after all. 'Prentice, it's hopeless!' There, she had called him by his first name, and she felt a twinge of pleasure when he looked up from his job and smiled at her. He had been formal on their first two meetings, so polite and yet so reserved—until he had lost his temper. Now, today, he seemed to have changed. Which was the real Prentice McCulloch? Did the cool veneer really hide a gentler nature than she had suspected?

'Look,' he said standing up straight, 'you're right. It is hopeless. I'll go back through the spinney with you and across the field. If we don't find it, then I'll get hold of a metal detector and try again.'

'Oh, please don't!' Dani bit her lip. She wanted her

watch back, and the thought of hurting her parents by admitting that she had lost it was an upsetting one. Yet she did not like the thought of being indebted to this man.

'Why not?' He stepped out of the stream. 'Don't you want it back?'

'Yes, of course. I just don't want to put you to a lot of trouble.' The excuse sounded weak and her voice tailed away.

'It's no trouble.' But a mask seemed to settle over his face, turning concern to bland indifference and vitality into bleak coldness. Dani was sorry. She had liked the sweet, warming smile he had given her and the casual way he had been grubbing about in a stream on her behalf. It was as if the sun had gone in and left her cold, and she resisted an impulse to wrap her arms around herself to protect her body from this man's chill.

'I appreciate all you're doing,' she said softly. 'I really do. But I know you're busy. I don't want to get in your way.'

'You already have.' He said the words stiffly, but one corner of his mouth tilted upwards into a grin. 'First you wake me up, then you lose your watch on my property. All in the space of a few hours.'

'I suppose so.' Dani felt awkward standing on the bank so close to him and watching as he took out a handkerchief and dried his hands. She did not know what to say to him; he inhibited her with the swift way he could change from starchy formality to easy friendliness so that she was never sure what effect her words would have on him. 'Can I help?' she asked, as he rubbed the sodden piece of material over his feet.

'Have you got a handkerchief?'

'Well . . .' She produced a tiny square of lace from her

pocket and then joined in the sudden peal of laughter that he uttered.

'All right.' He sat on the bank and pulled his socks on, wrestling them over his wet feet and then slipping into his shoes. 'I'll walk back with you and we'll have another look. Maybe we'll find it this time.'

'Yes.'

Dani liked the idea of a metal detector, and she wondered how she could hire one. She did not want to ask Prentice. She was really not sure if he was annoyed by the trouble she was causing him, and she did not want to risk his displeasure.

Side by side they walked through the spinney, and when Prentice's shoulder brushed against her own, Dani found it a comforting pressure. She had the most extraordinary feeling, without any rhyme or reason for it, that it would be nice to be holding his hand as they searched, and that this companionable sense of a common purpose might be extended if only she could find the right words.

Dani felt her stomach tie itself into a small, painful knot as the implication of her thoughts struck home. How could she think like that, she wondered dazedly? He was a stranger with whom she had nothing in common. This sense of peace between them was transitory and without substance.

Suddenly the sun seemed hotter than ever on her head and her body felt sticky as her shirt clung to her back, but she tried to ignore the discomfort. The closeness with him that she had felt just a few seconds before now seemed foolish and constricting. How could she feel so claustrophobic in the middle of a field?

'This is impossible.' Prentice stopped suddenly and straightened his back. Immediately Dani felt guilty.

'You're right,' she agreed. 'It is impossible.'

'I haven't said that I'm giving up.' He turned to look at her, and she tipped her face up and basked in the glow of his green eyes. 'We need a metal detector. Maybe two. I'll see to it.'

'Thank you. If you'll let me know what it all costs, I'll . . .' She made the offer awkwardly and knew immediately that it had been the wrong thing to say. His face changed to bleak wintriness and immediately he became the distant stranger. She took a deep breath and tried to qualify her statement. 'It is my watch,' she reminded him. 'And my fault for losing it.'

'True. All right, my lady, I'll send you the damn bill.' Clipped words forced through his teeth as if he hated to utter them.

'Now look . . .' Dani took a moment to marvel at how quickly this man could bring her temper to boiling point. She never lost patience with her children, and even when they were at their most exasperating, she was able to remain calm and sunny. Yet Prentice McCulloch made her feel as if a giant hand was ruffling her feathers the wrong way.

'Look at what?' He gave her no chance to finish what she was about to say. 'I offered to help. Just a simple gesture of neighbourliness. Why the hell are you people so damn unfriendly?'

'We aren't!' Dani defended her village. 'Maybe I'm just wondering why you're suddenly so helpful. Giving the grounds over to the fête, I can understand. That's good public relations. I don't know what you hope to gain by finding my watch.' She was appalled by her own words. She could not remember ever being so rude to anyone in her life before.

'I wasn't trying to gain anything.' The disgust in his voice pierced her like a flashing dagger. 'Still, with your teacher's salary and the money Brian pays you, you should be able to afford it. Sure, I'll send you the bill.' His lips twisted and Dani hated to see the ugly way it marred his generous mouth. 'Does he pay you more for stripping?' And then, as she digested the insult. 'Doesn't your boy-friend mind? Or is Brian the lucky man?'

Stunned, shocked, Dani was awed by the way his voice rose, by the vein that suddenly stood out at his jaw, and by the furious fire in the jade eyes. She felt seared by his words and scorched by the unfairness of them.

'How dare you!' It was all she could find to say, and her hands clenched into fists in frustration at the inadequacy of her words. 'How *dare* you!'

'Come on, schoolmarm, can't you do better than that?' The words were jeered, and Dani's fists clenched tighter. 'You were quick enough with your words a few minutes ago.'

Dani stared wide-eyed at the powerful, enraged man in front of her and felt the beginnings of a flood of words trembling on her lips. Deliberately she bit them back. He might not have the self-control to hold his temper, but she did.

'You,' she said, coldly and deliberately, 'aren't worth wasting words over. I'll claim the watch off my insurance company. Goodbye.' She nodded, turned and marched away, taking with her an impression of russet hair sparked with fire as the sun caught the red tints. She wondered vaguely if that was why he had such a temper.

Dani reached the stile and suddenly became aware of a rustle of movement beside her. Resolutely she refused to turn her head and look, but as she put one foot up on to the step, he jumped the fence next to it and stood waiting for her on the other side.

'Why do you annoy me?' He asked the question as she climbed decorously over the fence. 'I hate losing my temper and you make me do it so damn easily. Have you been taking lessons?'

'No.' Dani looked into his rueful face and resisted the desire to laugh. The anger had vanished just as quickly as it had appeared, and in its place was the half smile that she found so endearing. His lips were curved and suddenly she wondered what it would be like to lean forward and lay her own mouth against them. The thought frightened her. She could not afford involvement with this man. She couldn't!

'If I really wanted to annoy you,' she said, perching sedately on the top of the fence and trying to still the sudden thump of her heart, 'I'd tell you that I think you're a man with a get-rich-quick scheme and no thought for the beauty of what you're destroying so that you can make money.'

If he could be insulting, then so could she. Somehow she sensed he would be easier to deal with as an enemy rather than as anything else. Dani refused to ask herself what else he might be.

'You . . .' He looked as if he was choking back the words he wanted to use, and Dani watched him innocently, aware that she was playing with fire and tinglingly sure that it was dangerous; that he was dangerous. Being perched on the fence above him was, she decided, giving her only the illusion of being safe.

'Yes?' She asked temptingly as his voice did not seem to want to work. Let him be the enemy, she thought recklessly. At least that way she would know where she stood.

Arms reached out for her, hands grabbing her waist in a grip like a vice. She was pulled from her perch and felt the hard leanness of his body as he swung her down against him.

'Little schoolmarms aren't supposed to talk like that.' The words were whispered against her ear. 'But you're quite right. I'm annoyed.'

'Good.' She pushed against his chest to free herself, and waves of pulsing languor swept through her body as he refused to release her, holding her tightly and laughing softly when she thrust harder.

'What's the matter?' he asked tauntingly. 'If you play with fire, my lady, you're going to get burned one day.'

Dani hoped and prayed that no one was around to witness this little scene. The struggle was becoming undignified. He was far too strong for her, and his maleness was overpowering her resistance. He really was the enemy now.

'Let me go.' She tried to make the words into a command, tried to put the kind of authority into her voice that she used at school. He released her abruptly. 'You really should . . .' She took a deep breath to stop her voice from quivering. ' . . . exercise a little more self-control.'

'I appreciate the advice.' The volcanic temper was rising again. 'What is the matter with you? Been a spinster for too long? Or are you a natural shrew?'

It was so unfair! No one else roused her to these heights of anger. Dani compressed her lips into a straight line and glared at him.

'You really know how to get under my skin, don't you?' His voice was wondering. 'I don't think I need you in my life, Dani Robertson.'

'Believe me,' she flared, 'I don't need you in mine,

either. Not you or your plans for the Manor. Why did you come here?'

The last part was a cry of anger against the fates that had brought this tall, arrogant, flash-fire man to her village. She felt as if he was waking her up from a long sleep, dragging her—protesting and furious—out of her womb-like, smug complacency into a world of passionate emotions that she could not understand. He scared her.

'I'm beginning to wonder myself.' White temper lines appeared near his mouth. 'Does everyone get this kind of treatment or am I just one of the lucky ones?' He swung away from her. 'We'll just have to try to keep out of one another's way,' he said over his shoulder. 'Maybe if we do that we won't end up killing one another. I never . . .' He broke off, and dropped swiftly to one knee. Dani watched him, arms crossed defensively around her body to shield herself from his contempt, and then she gasped when he got to his feet again and something fragile and golden swung from between his thumb and forefinger. 'Look what I've got,' he said softly. 'Come here, my little wild-cat schoolmarm, and see what I've found.'

It was her watch. Dani took two paces forward and held out her hand, palm upwards.

'You've got it!' She could not contain her jubilation. 'Thank goodness for that. May I have it, please?'

'Oh . . . I don't know.' The watch dangled from his fingers, swinging slightly and drawing Dani's eyes hypnotically. 'What reward do I get?'

'Reward?' She did not take her gaze from the watch.

'Mmm. Don't I get a kiss for finding it?'

Dani felt her eyes flicker wide with shock. What was he? Demon, sorcerer, or just a man determined never to lose a shouting match with anyone, especially a woman.

'Please give me my watch,' she said steadily. 'I don't want to kiss you, and you don't want to be kissed.'

'What an honest lady!' He twisted the watch so that the gold caught the sun. 'How do you know I don't want you to kiss me?'

'Because . . .' Because if ever there was to be any kissing, Prentice McCulloch would want to make the moves himself.

'Yes?' he asked, in much the same tone she had used earlier to him.

'Don't play games,' she said. 'It's obvious that we should try to keep out of one another's way from now on, but don't make things any worse than they are. Please.' It was a last-ditch attempt to persuade him to give her the watch, and a last warning that her own temper was rising, fuelled by the still-remembered insults and the slow-burning implication of his opinion of her. 'Please.'

He threw back his head and laughed. She watched him dispassionately, noting the even white teeth and the long sweep of his throat. He had resented the fact that she could anger him and could find the words to answer his taunts. Now he knew that he had the upper hand and he was enjoying himself.

'Come and get it then.' He looked at her, looked deep into her eyes, and his magnetism caught her and held her. 'Come on, schoolmarm . . . come and get your watch.'

Fury threatened to choke her. She took a step forward and he took a step back. She took another step, and again his long legs carried him away from her. Then she saw the soft, marshy bank of the pond give way a little under his weight. She closed the gap between them quickly and snatched the watch from his outstretched hand. The bank subsided even more as he tried to throw his weight towards the firmer ground, and for a moment he teetered helplessly on a see-saw of precarious balance.

One push. That was all it would take. One push in the wrong direction. Dare she?

Dani pushed him.

CHAPTER FOUR

THE Manor looked beautiful. Dani smiled affectionately as she turned her Fiesta into the main driveway of the house and saw it lying before her, basking like a great stone cat in the heat of the summer sun. The mellow bricks seemed to be soaking up the warmth, and the windows reflected back the light and shone with a diamond-like brilliance that was dazzling.

Long and low and old, the Manor was at its best on this summer's afternoon. Girded by trim, neatly cut lawns and tidy paths, garlanded with ivy, the Manor was *en fête*, and all the brightly decorated stalls on the front lawns added a touch of gaiety in a medley of coloured bunting and streamers and ribbons. The two huge cedar trees, one set in the centre of each lawn on either side of the main driveway, seemed more majestic than ever, and under their canopied branches the village prepared to enjoy itself, while the Manor looked on with benevolent interest.

Dani parked the car and made her way to the area allocated to her puppet show under one of the cedar trees. Originally, it was to have been a Punch and Judy show, but she had never really liked the traditional story, and had childhood memories of being terrified by the crocodile. So she had created a new story, with the aid of one of her friends, and the handmade glove puppets now lay in their box waiting for the first performance.

Dani strolled across the short grass towards the booth

61

looking around her for Les Whelen, the local vet, who was her co-puppeteer. She could not see him, but attached to the green, white and blue striped material of the booth she found a note in his almost decipherable scrawl.

'Oh no!' The two of them had spent hours practising the play and now he had been called to a farm thirty miles away. He could be gone for the whole afternoon, in fact his note recommended Dani to find someone to take his place.

She could not do it on her own. Often the script called for three characters to be on stage at once and she only had two hands. Yet most of the village people already had jobs of their own to do, and none of the children in the school were quite tall enough. Maybe she could get a box for one of them.

Possible ideas crowded her mind as she stared around at the other stalls. There were a large number of them. The village was small, but its inhabitants were enthusiastic people and the fête was one of the highlights of their year. Dani scanned the white elephant stall, the cake stall, the W.I. stall, the second-hand toy stall, and let her eyes run over the grass beyond them. Was there no one who did not already have a job to do?

'Looking for someone?'

The voice was horribly familiar. Dani felt her heart give a great lurch and turned to stare at Prentice McCulloch. She had been aware of him all day, seeing him busy with the personal address system looking casual but workmanlike in blue jeans and a navy T-shirt. She had kept out of his way, hoping that he would see her and emulate her example. It seemed that he could not. Now he stood before her in black cord trousers and a snowy white shirt open at the neck. He watched her unsmilingly.

'I thought you'd make it your business to be a thousand

miles away from here today,' she ventured, and the
circumstances of their last meeting made her voice wobble
nervously.

'Actually, I only came to see that my lawns weren't
completely ruined.' He drew on a thin cigar he was
smoking and flicked ash towards the roots of the cedar
tree. 'But then an enthusiastic lady roped me in to set up
the skittle alley, and after that,' he shrugged, 'well, somehow after that I got involved. It's a damn nuisance but
there you are. Anything you want me to do?'

The last time she had seen him to speak to, he had been
dragging himself out of a green, evil-smelling, slime-
covered pond. He had been uttering obscenities that
should have made Dani blush, but which had not because
she had been laughing so hard. Yes, she had laughed at
him. Now, as she faced him again, she wondered at her own
temerity. A man like Prentice McCulloch would never
forgive her. This had to be the calm before the storm.

'I don't think so,' she said uncertainly.

'Are you sure? You wouldn't like me to be an Aunt
Sally?' He jerked his thumb towards the game, always
popular, that involved throwing balls at a target. When
the target was struck cleanly, a bucket of water descended
on the hapless victim waiting below.

'No, thanks.' Dani's lips twitched in amusement.

'I got very wet the last time we met,' he said casually,
hooking his thumbs into the hip pockets of his trousers
and tilting his face up to the sky. 'I'm glad you enjoyed
yourself.'

'I'm sorry I laughed,' Dani answered meekly, and
embarrassment made her clear her throat before the
words could be uttered.

'Me too.' He still seemed to be contemplating the tree

above his head. 'You don't conform to my image of school teachers. The ones I know don't push people into duckponds.'

'The men *I* know don't insult me,' she snapped back tartly. 'You asked for what you got.'

'I did?' He shifted his gaze and green eyes locked with hers. 'Well . . . maybe I did.' A crooked half-smile lifted one corner of his mouth. 'Why don't we call a truce?'

No, oh no, that was much too easy. Prentice McCulloch was not the kind of man to allow anyone to get the better of him. Dani hesitated.

'All right,' she said quietly, but she resolved never to let her guard down when she was with him. Never. He had all the instincts of an expert duellist. He would fence with her, and he would attack when she least expected it. He would never forget her mocking laughter or the way she had sprinted from him with the watch clasped triumphantly in her hand.

'So . . . is there anything I can do for you?' Prentice smiled and, as once before, Dani was captivated by the sweetness of it. If only she could be sure it was genuine! 'Since I seem to have got involved in all this, I may as well make the best of it.'

'Could you talk like a dragon?' Who else could she ask? They only just had enough people to man all the stalls, and even some of the older children in the school were helping. The fête always drew hundreds of people from the surrounding villages and was generally judged to be one of the best in the area.

'Talk like a what?' His well-shaped eyebrows shot upwards.

'A dragon. Look . . .' She walked around to the back of the booth and opened the big box that sat on a trestle table. Carefully she drew out a large green, black and yellow dragon with a silly expression on its face. '. . . here he is. I'm doing a puppet show for the children.' Dani shrugged. 'Les Whelen was supposed to help me, but he's been called away.' She held out the dragon to Prentice who took it carefully and examined it. 'It's based on the story of George and the Dragon,' she explained, nervous that he would turn her down. 'I've added to the original story so that it isn't the same as the legend. You'd have to talk for Saint George too, and do a couple of the minor characters.'

'Did you make this?' He was still turning the puppet over in his hands.

'Yes.' She was secretly pleased with her dragon. Vicious looking spines marched down his back, and his tail had a very satisfactory look of power about it, but the laughing expression of the monster made him seem less fearsome.

'It's beautiful.' He found out how to slip it on and suddenly the dragon was not an inanimate puppet but a miniature fire-breather. 'Do you want me to talk like this?' He dropped his voice to a bass, growly rumble. 'Or shall we go for something more avant-garde?' He raised his voice, found the string that operated the dragon's eyelids, and batted them coyly at her. Dani laughed.

'That first voice,' she said. 'It's good. You surprise me.'

'Why?' Guileless green eyes met hers and Dani hesitated, torn between wanting to confess that she had not realised that he had a sense of humour, and miserably aware of what had happened the last time they had met.

'Not everyone can do it well,' she temporised quickly. 'Do you want to read through the script?'

'If I'm going to do it, I think perhaps I'd better.'

Dani handed him the typed sheets of paper and began to get the puppets out of their box. Saint George, the sun glinting off his metal sword and shield, the Lady Lucinda with her long, blonde hair and brocade dress, the horse which was modelled on a pantomime horse and followed Saint George everywhere, and the minor characters. She was very conscious of Prentice at her elbow as she put them in their correct order of use and straightened their costumes, and when she told him which ones would be his, and he began to practise some of the voices quietly, she hid a grin.

'You know, these really are very good,' Prentice said. He began to pick up the puppets that he would be using, trying them on and working them experimentally. 'I think you've missed your vocation. They must have taken you hours and hours to make.'

'Yes, they did.' They had filled in the long winter evenings when she had sat on the floor of her flat with them and agonised over how she could make the horse's jaw move, and how to make the dragon's eyelids work. Some of her friends had helped with materials and sewing, and it had been Brian who had finally resolved the problem of the eyelids and jaw. 'But I enjoyed it.' They seemed to have left the incident of the pond behind and Dani was glad.

'What will you do with them when this is all over?' Prentice put Saint George down and lifted the dragon again. It seemed to be his favourite.

'I really don't know. Use them again next year, perhaps.'

'That's a pity. They should be displayed somewhere. They really are superb.'

The praise was genuine, Dani was sure of that, and she felt colour creep into her cheeks at the open admiration in his voice. She ducked her head so that he should not see the blush and took a moment to wonder why he could so easily make her feel emotional. She picked up the horse hurriedly to mask her confusion and it slipped out of her hands. She made an ineffectual grab for it, found Prentice's hands there too, and between them they saved the horse from falling to the ground.

'Whew!' Dani let her breath out in a gasp of relief. 'Thanks.'

Somehow Prentice's fingers were all mixed up with hers as they both retained a grip on the puppet. Dani felt the warmth of his skin, the strength that he seemed to manage to hide so well, and she was even aware of the fine hairs that sprinkled the back of his hand.

'Will you take him or shall I?' His voice interrupted her exploration of the sense of touch and she dropped her eyelashes so that he should not see her expression.

'I've got him.' She grasped the puppet firmly and his fingers slid away, but slowly as if he was as reluctant to break the contact as she was. As the thought crossed Dani's mind, she glanced involuntarily up at him and in the swift movement she caught sight of a look of intensity in his face. Then it was gone and he grinned at her.

'Can we run through this?' he asked. 'So that I know exactly what I'm doing?'

'Of course.'

Dani was surprised and delighted with the amount of concentration that Prentice put into his attempt to master the puppets and absorb the script. Some people, she knew, might not have thought it important if there was a hitch in the play, but he wanted it perfect and Dani admired his determination.

'Okay,' he said at last. 'I think I've got the hang of some of it now. Can we try out the booth?'

'Yes, that's a good idea.'

Prentice held the back flap of the tent-like structure open while Dani positioned the puppets and kicked off her high-heeled sandals, then he let it drop and came to stand beside her. At once it became obvious that the top of his head could be seen from outside and Dani clicked her tongue in disappointment.

'You're too tall,' she said disconsolately. 'I'd forgotten that. Les is an inch taller than me and I'm only five foot six. You must be over six feet.'

'Around that,' he admitted. 'How about this?'

He bent his knees until his face was level with Dani's. She had never been so close to him before, and in the sultry dimness of their confinement, his eyes gleamed like a cat's.

'It takes nearly half an hour to get through,' she said helplessly. 'You'll never be able to stay like that.'

'Do you have a better idea?' His lips formed the words and Dani stared at them as though mesmerised. He was just too close. Their shoulders were touching, he had to turn his body slightly to fit his length into the narrowness of the booth, and his face was so close to hers that she could feel the warmth of his breath on her cheek.

'No,' she admitted honestly. 'I don't.'

'Well then . . .' He shrugged slightly. 'I'll have to put up with it.'

Dani wondered why she had never noticed before how cramped the booth was. Certainly Les Whelen was only about her height and very slim, but Prentice seemed like a giant in the land of Lilliput as he tried to adjust his height and turn round a little more so that he could reach his puppets.

'Oh, this is impossible!' she burst out. 'You can't do it, Prentice. You'll get cramp . . .'

'I can do it.' There was steely determination in his voice. 'If you could have got someone else then I'd have been the last person you'd have asked. Right?'

'Right,' she admitted, and she shifted a little in the booth to try and put a little distance between them, banging her arm sharply on the shelf as she did so. She bit back a yelp of pain and heard him smother a laugh. 'It isn't funny!' she snapped. 'I'm just trying to give you some more room.'

'Oh, yeah?' He drawled the words. 'Don't worry, I'm fine. I'm quite enjoying it, in fact. What could be more fun than spending a summer afternoon in a tent that's more like a sauna with a pretty puppeteer?' Laughter lines appeared at the corners of his eyes and she stared at him uncertainly, totally unsure of whether he was being sarcastic or if he really meant what he said.

'We have to do the play twice,' she warned. 'Once in about fifteen minutes time and then again in an hour and a half. Are you sure that you . . .'

'I've told you I can!' This time the snap was quite unmistakable. 'I do appreciate the fact that you'd rather have your vet friend in here with you, but it's not my fault if he'd rather look at a sick cow.' In his annoyance just a hint of a Scottish brogue appeared in his voice. Dani noticed it, liked it, and spoke placatingly.

'Actually, it's a horse. And he has a wife and two children. I'm only thinking of you . . .'

'Well, don't. You concentrate on what you're supposed

to be doing, Miss Robertson, and I'll get out of here for ten minutes and go through that script again.'

Miss Robertson. Dani opened her mouth to explain, belatedly, that she was Mrs Robertson, but he was gone, ducking out of the back of the tent without another word. When she peered out after him, he was striding in the direction of the house, the script flapping in his hand and his long legs covering the ground rapidly.

She was going to have to endure more than an hour in his presence, cooped up in a confined space with him and his inflammatory temper. Dani took a deep breath and tried to steady herself. If it had been any other occasion, any other occasion at all, she would have turned coward and refused to go on, but there was no excuse that she could offer, and the thought that her puppets might never be used at all made her set her jaw firmly and decide to go through with it.

She stepped out of the booth for a breath of air. It had been hot inside; hot and airless and stifling. She and Les had practised the play many times before, but never on such a day. The canvas seemed to be attracting the heat and Dani leaned against the trunk of the cedar tree and closed her eyes. She could feel a prickle of perspiration on her forehead and upper lip and even the brevity of her pale yellow sundress with its string-like straps that fastened into two bows at her shoulders and showed off the faint tan she had acquired was not helping her to feel cool. A bikini would be more suitable for the atmosphere inside the tent. She fanned herself with her own copy of the script and prayed that Les might return unexpectedly.

There were to be no miracles that day. When the personal address system announced the attraction of the puppet show and she slipped reluctantly back inside the booth, Prentice McCulloch was beside her as she wriggled her hand into the first puppet.

Not a word was spoken as he picked up Saint George and one of the minor characters and laid his script on the shelf, but she was nervously aware of stage-fright as she checked her own assortment of puppets for the last time. Prentice was unprepared, whereas she and Les had practised for hours with the vet's wife coaching them from the front of the booth. He could do the voices but he had not had a chance to practise the movements of the puppets above his head as he worked them, and a thousand things could go wrong.

'Good luck!' She did not really want to talk to him, but the words were out before she could stop them. 'We'll just have to do the best we can.'

'Don't know about your best, lady, but mine's pretty good.' He drawled the words without looking at her, but she raised an eyebrow at his confidence and sighed inwardly.

'You'll have to shout,' she said warningly. 'Don't forget.'

'Yes, ma'am.'

'And if your arms get tired, you can rest your elbows on the ledge.'

'Naturally.'

'I am trying,' she hissed furiously, 'to help.'

'Thanks very much.'

Dani wanted to hit him. Never before had she experienced such a red rush of anger, and never before had one person so infuriated her. She had a sudden vision of the two of them engaging in a furious battle inside the tent and everyone outside watching as the booth rocked and swayed. Immediately the anger vanished and she had to choke down a bubble of laughter. Anxious laughter. She had never attempted anything like this before and although she could not be seen by the audience, she was fully aware that most people knew who was working the puppets.

'Ready?' Her voice came out as a nervous squeak.

'Yes.' He turned to look at her then, their faces only a few inches apart, and Dani saw the pearling of sweat on his forehead. Lord, but it was hot! 'Good luck.' He winked, suddenly and unexpectedly, and she was close enough to see that his eyelashes were as long and black and thick as her own. She nodded to acknowledge his words and then pulled on the cord that would raise the curtain.

It had only been running for five minutes when Dani realised that she had seriously underestimated Prentice. His Saint George was truly heroic and the voices he gave to his minor characters were better than anything Les Whelen had attempted. His confidence and his apparent mastery both of the script and his puppets inspired Dani. Instead of being nervous for both of them, she ceased to worry about his performance and concentrated on making her own equal to his. Lady Lucinda was a breathless, tremulous heroine and the pantomime horse rasied laughter every time it put in an appearance.

After ten minutes Dani knew that the audience were on their side, and that the laughter was all coming in the right places. She relaxed a little and began to enjoy herself, marvelling at the smoothness of the performance and even grinning a little as she put up the horse again and heard the ripple of applause that greeted his entrance. She moved him along the stage a little so that he was following Saint George, and her arm brushed along Prentice's side.

It was like being jolted by electricity. She was conscious of taking a deep breath and of pulling her arm away, but now she was forced to acknowledge that she could feel the heat of his body and the vitality in it as if they were pressed closely together.

He was watching her. She spoke her lines automatically, but in the gloom of the booth she could see that he was smiling, his teeth very white in his tanned face, his jade eyes knowing and full of laughter. He held her eyes with his own and she was powerless to look away, but instead was forced to stare into them until she felt as though the sea had her in a strong undercurrent and was pulling her down and down into its inviting depths. His eyes were the sea and she was happily drowning.

'The dragon!' It was a life-saver and she clung to it. 'Let me help you . . .' and she dragged her gaze away and assisted him to fit it on to his hand, drawing the green material up his arm and straightening out a bent spine. The hairs on Prentice's arm were soft and silky, and suddenly she was again in danger of being sucked out to sea by that innocent touch of her fingers on his skin. The inside of his elbow, bare and vulnerable, drew her strangely and she would have laughed at her own silliness if she had not felt so impossibly drawn to him.

Impulsively, without thinking about it, she pulled her handkerchief from her pocket and mopped his face with it. He was working hard, and the strain of having to bend his back and still manoeuvre the puppets above his head, was beginning to tell. He looked hot, and the gentle side of her nature felt sorry for him. His eyes thanked her and then the dragon made his appearance.

Prentice made him slink on from the side of the stage, working his arm at an incredibly uncomfortable angle to get the right effect, and Dani tilted her head backwards so that she could see what he was doing. She should have thought of bringing him on from the side like that. It was remarkably effective and Prentice's voice, when he made the dragon talk, was a wonder of gruffness.

If only they weren't so close. Alternatively, if only they knew one another better so that she could show her admiration by squeezing his free hand or saying something to him that he would not misunderstand. On impulse, when Lady Lucinda made her next entrance, Dani added a touch of hero-worship to the puppet's voice.

At this stage of the play they had to work two puppets apiece, and Dani had no choice but to brush against Prentice as one of her characters moved across the stage. His body felt as hard and firm as it had looked when he had been sitting up in bed on that memorable morning, and when she leaned a little further towards him and he tried to shift his frame to make way for her, she heard a stifled laugh close to her neck.

'This is bad management,' he whispered as he allowed her to duck under his left arm. 'Can't you keep to your own side?'

'No,' she muttered back, and then she gave her attention to the Lady Lucinda again, cursing Les Whelen's wife who had thought the changeover would be appreciated by the adults watching, who would know that the puppeteers were working in a confined space. She had also said that it would make the puppets more realistic to be moved from one side of the stage to the other. With Les it had worked perfectly well, but Prentice had not anticipated the move, and Dani realised suddenly that she was blocking the script from his sight. The Lady Lucinda moved smartly back to her own side of the stage, but not before Dani had

been unable to avoid brushing against Prentice's body
again, and as she said her lines, she recalled vividly the
feel of the muscles of his thigh and his arm as she had
squeezed by him.

When had she last been stirred by the proximity of a
man? Dani could not remember. Nor could she recall a
time when her pulses had raced so fast or when she had felt
suddenly and unaccountably nervous and shy.

What did she have to say next? The loss of concentration put her next speech out of her head, and when she
glanced down at her own copy of the script, she saw that
she had forgotten to turn over the page. Both her hands
were occupied, and even when she closed her eyes for a
second and thought desperately, she could not remember
her lines.

Prentice's script! She leaned over to look at it and once
again he had to move to make room for her. Now she could
feel his breath on her cheek again, and as she found her
place and read the lines, she felt his mouth touch her ear.

It was so unexpected, so totally and utterly unlike the
Prentice McCulloch that she thought she knew that for a
moment her mind went blank again. All she could feel was
the light pressure of his lips against the curve of her ear
and then the tingling warmth as he worked his way down
to her neck. This wasn't happening! Wildly Dani wondered how she was supposed to concentrate on her lines
while this disconcerting, arrogant man was nuzzling the
soft, vulnerable spot just above her collarbone.

They had almost finished. This was Lady Lucinda's
last speech before Saint George closed the play. Dani
wanted to pull away from Prentice but there simply was
no room and anyway, she rationalised, he would have to
stop this oddly exciting teasing when his turn came to

speak. When his mouth moved away she was both relieved and disappointed.

Lady Lucinda finished her speech rather breathlessly
and Dani relaxed, waiting now for the final action of the
play when the two puppets would embrace. One more
minute and she could push her way out of the back of the
booth and the stifling heat could be left behind her for a
while. And so could the closeness of Prentice McCulloch.

The stage now had only the two principal characters on
it. Dani wriggled her hand free of the second puppet and
when Prentice held his arm out mutely, she stripped the
puppet of the Blue Knight from his hand and put it aside.
Just a few more moments, a few more seconds, and she
could break free of this man's disturbing presence and
calm her chaotic heartbeat.

His hand was touching her jaw, turning her towards
him. Wonderingly Dani looked into his face and saw that
same expression of curious intentness that she had glimpsed earlier. Prentice finished what he had to say, Dani
moved her puppet closer for the final embrace, and then
Prentice's face was coming towards her own and his free
hand was cupping the back of her head to prevent her
moving away. Then his mouth closed over hers.

Dani had never been kissed like that before. Not with
that kind of single-minded purpose, not with that kind of
thoroughness or that hint of muted passion that she
thought she sensed behind the firm lips that were waking
dormant sensations and desires inside her that she had
long forgotten. His lips moved over hers with a careful
gentleness as if, for once in his ordered life, he was not sure
how she would respond, and after a moment's hesitation
in which she was passive and unresisting, she allowed the
barriers to fall a little and kissed him back.

Lady Lucinda and Saint George moved closer to emulate the actions of their masters. Prentice's hand moved down Dani's back to slide around her waist, drawing her closer to the hardness of that male body that she had been so nervous of earlier, and she raised her hand and shyly and tentatively touched his shoulder as the kiss lengthened and deepened until Dani became aware of nothing but his mouth and his arm and the incredible heat that emanated from him. It was Prentice who, with great presence of mind, lowered the curtain on the hero and heroine on stage.

'I think you owed me this.' He released her lips just long enough to make the statement and then claimed them again.

'I did?' Dani's question was an incoherent mumble.

'Yes, you did.' His lips traced a path from her mouth up across her cheek to her eyelid, feathering across the soft surface and making her tremble. 'I found your watch, remember?'

'Mmm.'

Dani tried to tell herself not to be so flustered by a single kiss. It was a temporary closeness in the heat of the moment, a release from tension because the play had gone so well, a fleeting encounter with an attractive man.

She denied the thought even as it crossed her mind. It was more than that to her. She had come alive under his touch, and had felt warm and glowing and vital. Now, as he stepped back, she felt it all fading away leaving her drained and miserable. Why, oh why had he kissed her? It would have been so much better if he had remained distant and formal.

The people outside were applauding. For a second Dani

and Prentice looked at one another and she was held spellbound by the expression in his eyes. Then he was holding up the back flap of the tent, catching her hand and pulling her out with him.

'Go and take a bow.' His face was alight with laughter and triumph that they had done so well.

Dani obeyed him without question, going around to the front of the booth and, hands held awkwardly behind her back, face going pink, she smiled at the people who were clapping. She did not like to be the centre of attention, not like this, not when she could still feel the pressure of Prentice's mouth on hers and the strength and security of the embrace in which she had just been held. Couldn't everyone see that she had been kissed and was still reeling from the pleasure of it?

One more nervous smile and then she could escape. She had been aware of Prentice's eyes on her back as she stood in front of the booth, but when she turned impulsively, meaning to bring him forward and explain his part in the show, she saw that he had gone and the disappointment inside her was keen and biting.

'Mrs Robertson . . .' Her attention was claimed by one of her children. ' . . . that was ace, Mrs Robertson!' Ace was the most popular word in the school and Dani heard it fifty times a day. Yet she still appreciated the compliment and when more of her children crowded around her and asked about the puppets, she took them around to the back of the booth and drew out the dragon.

'Make him wink, Mrs Robertson,' another child begged, and with an inward sigh Dani abandoned the idea of finding herself a cold drink and relaxing until the next performance and settled herself on the grass to demonstrate her handiwork, making the dragon wink at one little girl.

'Do the growly voice,' the first child, Darren, said insistently.

'Darren, I can't. That was Mr McCulloch, not me. I can't make my voice go that deep.'

'Try. Please!'

'All right.' She lowered her voice and attempted to imitate Prentice's rendition of the dragon's gruffness, leaning back against the trunk of the cedar tree and tucking her feet to one side as an over-enthusiastic child fell over them in an attempt to get closer.

'That's a super hat, Sally!' She spied a baseball cap, obviously meant for an adult, that almost obscured the face of one of her pupils. 'Where did you get it?'

'White elephant stall, miss.' Sally took it off and held it out. 'D'you want to try it on?'

'Yes, please.' It was even too big for Dani's head, but she stuck it jauntily on the back and then impulsively held out her hand to Sally's three-year-old brother. Nicholas had always been a secret favourite of hers from the time he had sat up in his pram and favoured her with a great, toothless grin. He was more shy with her now, but she found him powerfully endearing and when he came to sit on her lap, propelled by his more outgoing sister, she snuggled his sturdy body against her own and made the dragon wink at him, too.

'I've brought you a drink.'

Startled, she looked up and saw Prentice standing on the edge of her group. He looked taller than ever from her sitting position on the grass, and she was suddenly and acutely aware of the baseball cap perched on the back of her head, of the small boy in her lap, and the way the children were clamouring for her attention.

'Thank you.' She extricated her arm from around

Nicholas's waist and prepared to stand up.

'Please . . . just one more wink!' The irrepressible Darren again, and at once the other children took up the request.

'Please . . . please, Mrs Robertson.'

'Just once more.' She made the dragon wink very slowly and very deliberately three times and then set Nicholas back on his feet. 'Go and find your parents,' she told the children. 'If I don't have a drink then I won't have any voice left for the rest of the afternoon.'

The children moved away obediently, one or two of them casting curious glances at the big man who was occupying their teacher's attention, and Dani scrambled up from the grass and held out her hand for the drink.

'Thank you,' she said warmly. 'I think you've saved my life!' Impishly she raised the glass a little to toast him and then saw the frozen look on his face. 'Have you seen a ghost?' she asked lightly. 'Prentice?'

'Mrs Robertson.' He laid great emphasis on the title. 'I didn't know you were Mrs Robertson.' Again the stress on the one word.

'It isn't a secret,' Dani told him. 'Didn't you know?' Of course he hadn't known. She bit her lip at the stupidity of her question and stared helplessly into the cold, green eyes.

'No.' The one word was a curt bark of sound. 'I don't make a practice of kissing married women . . . or are you a widow?' Dani wondered if she imagined the slight lift in his voice, as if the thought had only just occurred to him.

'No,' she said quietly. 'I'm not a widow.'

As though it was coming from a great distance, she heard the noise of the fête all around her; children shouting, the start of the music as the Morris dancers came out to perform, the click of the wooden skittles as someone tried their hand at winning a pig, and the almost inaudible voice of Harry as he announced the finding of a purse on the grass.

None of it was important. Nothing was important but the stony face of the man in front of her, who was looking at her and through her as if she no longer existed for him. But she did! She was the girl he had kissed just a few minutes before. She had not changed in anyone's eyes but his.

What was he thinking? Dani wondered frantically. That she was a wife who went around kissing other men in her husband's absence? Yes, that was probably it. The contempt was there in his face, as was the disillusionment and the sudden weary knowledge that he had been wrong about her.

'Let me explain,' she began quietly.

'I don't want to hear!' Brusquely, arrogantly, he turned aside her faltered words. 'What time is the next performance? Three-quarters of an hour? I'll be back . . . Mrs Robertson.'

He turned and walked away, and Dani suddenly remembered the ridiculous hat and snatched it off, wanting to cry and biting her lip against the tears. With this man she could do nothing right.

CHAPTER FIVE

DANI eased her Ford Fiesta into its parking space at the side of the barn and locked it securely. Her puppets were in the back but they would just have to stay there for the night. The box in which they lay was heavy and cumbersome and she did not feel equal to the task of carrying it up her flight of stairs.

She could not remember the last time she had felt so tired, and equally she could not understand the reason for it. It wasn't an ordinary, yawning kind of tiredness, but a bone-deep weariness that was making her reluctant even to cross the yard and ascend her stairs.

'Dani!' Brian's voice. As she turned slowly around, he opened the window of the studio and leaned out. 'You want a cup of coffee?'

'Yes, please.' She had drunk innumerable cups of tea and lemonade and the thought of the company was more appealing than the offer of a drink. She checked that the boot of the car was locked, picked up her handbag from the roof and walked slowly into Brian's flat, kicking off her shoes and carrying them in her hand as soon as she crossed the threshold.

She did not know why on earth she had gone to the fête in such ridiculously high-heeled sandals. Because she had hoped to see Prentice McCulloch and impress him with her sophistication? Well, she had seen him, and now she did not want to think about him. She still felt bruised from the icy look of scorn with which he had withered her before turning away, and from the miserable, stressed half hour that she had been forced to spend with him in the close confines of the play booth during the second performance of her puppets.

Dani knew that she never wanted to endure anything like that again. He had said nothing, absolutely nothing, but she had been made fully aware of his disapproval, and in the end her unhappiness had turned to a deep, burning anger. They should have kept to their original agreement to stay away from one another. It would have saved her from this latest hurtful incident.

Goodbye Prentice McCulloch, Dani thought as she padded across the wooden floor, settled herself down on Brian's couch-cum-bed and wriggled her feet blissfully into a sheepskin rug, nice to have met you. What was she going to do when they met again? No, she was just too tired to worry about that now.

'I've put the coffee on.' Brian came out of the kitchen and Dani looked up at him. 'My dear girl, you look as if you've been through a mincer. Was the fête that bad?'

'Not really.'

'Would you rather have a brandy now and your coffee later?'

'Oh, yes please.' Maybe she would find the strength to crawl upstairs to her own flat with some alcohol inside her.

She watched Brian as he went over to an old Welsh dresser where he kept his glasses and bottles. In old shorts that had obviously, at some stage, been jeans before he had cut the legs off and left the ends to fray, and a navy-blue T-shirt with the name of an American university emblazoned across it, he looked as powerful and as male as his half-brother. And yet Dani knew that she was not drawn to him in the way his half-brother attracted her.

But why? Brian's body was as well-proportioned and tanned as his brother's. Brian wore his clothes with the same casualness as Prentice. Brian was, in his way, just as attractive. Yet Dani tested her emotions and felt nothing for him. Why, oh why, did it have to be Prentice who stirred her blood and made her feel weak? Of all men, why him?

'One large brandy coming up.' Brian turned with her glass in his hand. 'If the other organisers look like you, they'll be bringing them home on stretchers.'

'I think I must have a summer cold coming.' Dani knew there was no real reason for her tiredness. Many of the other women were older than she was and had done more than she had done. She held out her hand for the drink and was surprised when Brian did not give it to her immediately' but clasped her hand in both of his.

'You're cold!' he exclaimed. 'Here – I'll get a jacket.'

'Don't fuss, Brian.' And yet she appreciated his concern and felt safe and protected in his flat away from Prentice's anger. She took her glass and sipped at the brandy.

'Is there some kind of bug going around the school?' Brian fetched a big, woolly cardigan in bright red and an equally bright blue. Dani winced. 'Yes,' Brian sighed. 'I don't like it either. But it'll get you warm. You want something to eat? An omelette?'

Apart from a few sandwiches and a sausage roll, Dani had eaten nothing all day. She nodded.

'There is an ulterior motive to all this fatherly concern,' Brian called as he went into the kitchen. 'I want you to sit for me tomorrow and I don't want to have to tie you to a broom handle to keep you upright. You want cheese or ham in your omelette?'

'Cheese, please.'

'Yes, madam.' Brian popped his head around the door and grinned at her. 'Help yourself to another brandy,' he invited her. 'If you keel over, I can always pour you upstairs to bed.'

'You're too kind!'

'Aren't I just?'

Dani did not have the energy to get up. She pulled the thick cardigan more closely around her and lifted her legs on to the couch, curling her feet under her and half sitting, half lying on the comfortable mattress. The brandy and the cardigan were warming her, and as the effect of the alcohol began to ease away the jumpy state of her nerves, she mused for a minute on the strangeness of human relationships.

She liked Brian. She thought he liked her. Yet she felt absolutely nothing for him beyond a kind of sisterly gratitude that he was looking after her. Neither was he attracted to her. He was too open to be able to hide his feelings and, besides that, Dani knew that he was more than halfway in love with his girlfriend Tricia, while still proclaiming his bachelor independence.

Prentice McCulloch was different. She felt she understood Brian, but his half-brother was an enigma to her. She suspected that Prentice hid his emotions behind that polite veneer of his and that perhaps few people would be allowed to see behind the mask to the man she thought lurked beneath it. She had been allowed peeps of a different Prentice. A man with the most beautiful smile she had ever seen, a man with a temper that could erupt suddenly and explosively, and a man who had treated a children's puppet show as if it had been as important as a big business deal.

Now she knew what it was like to be kissed by him, and she wondered if she would ever forget. She had felt physical warmth and an inner fire that he had lit with just one touch of his lips. Would his loving be as fierce and intense as his temper? Did he give to others the tenderness that he had shown her he possessed? Despite the cardigan and the brandy Dani shivered, recalling the ice in the green eyes after the revelation that she was Mrs Robertson. He would also make a cold, deadly and implacable enemy.

'Your brother found out that I was Mrs Robertson today,' she called to Brian.

'Oh yes?' He came to the kitchen door, a palette knife in one hand and a butcher's apron wrapped around his waist. 'What did he say?'

'Nothing much.' Dani fiddled with her brandy glass. 'But he didn't like it.'

'I don't suppose he did.' Brian went back into the kitchen but his voice still reached her. 'He doesn't like any divorced woman . . . no matter what the reason. Because of his own mother, I suppose.'

'Yes.' Brian was only confirming what Dani had suspected. 'But I didn't actually tell him that I was divorced. I didn't get a chance.'

'You aren't wearing a wedding ring,' Brian called out. 'I expect he can put two and two together. Tell him straight next time you see him.'

'I don't see any point.' Dispiritedly, Dani gulped at her brandy.

'Don't you?' Brian came back to the door of the room. 'You can't avoid him, Dani. He's going to be a part of the village now.'

'Whose side are you on?' Dani demanded, aware that

the alcohol and the tiredness were loosening her tongue. 'I didn't think you liked him either.' She finished her brandy with a defiant gulp and coughed.

'I didn't.' Bland agreement as Brian disappeared back into the kitchen. 'Just let me finish this and then I'll tell you . . .'

Five minutes later, Dani accepted the fluffy-looking omelette and a fork and waved it in mock threat at him.

'You didn't like him,' she stated definitely. 'Have you changed your mind?'

'I suppose so,' Brian admitted. He got himself a beer and sat cross-legged on the floor at her feet. 'Remember that morning you found him sleeping here?'

'I've been meaning to ask you about that.'

'Yes? Well, he came over the night before just for a beer. He had . . .' Brian's face bore an impish, reminiscent smile, '. . . quite a few in the end. I got him to talk about his childhood and how he felt about the world in general, and . . .' Now the smile became rueful. ' . . . hell, I felt sorry for him. I think he's been lonely all his life. Lots of people always round him, but still lonely. He's an honest man and I like him for it. Apart from his father, I don't think he's ever been close to anyone. We got along well, better than I ever thought we could. Anyway . . .' Abruptly Brian reverted to Dani's original topic. ' . . . all you have to do when you see him next is to tell him that you aren't married any more. At least he'll know where he stands.'

'I think he already does.' Sadly, Dani remembered that cold look of scorn. 'The only thing I can do is to keep out of his way.'

'If that's what you want,' Brian said neutrally. The rap on the front door startled them both, and he scowled. 'Bit late for a social call.' He glanced at his watch. 'Eat your omelette, Dani-girl, and I'll see who it is.'

It was Prentice. Dani had guessed that from the moment she heard the knocking, because it was so typical of the man himself. Decisive. She had a moment to prepare herself, but he obviously did not suspect her presence until he saw her.

'Oh,' he said. 'I didn't realise you'd be here. Am I interrupting something, Brian?' His voice was polite, but Dani met the frosty green eyes and shivered.

'No.' Brian's bright eyes went from his brother to Dani and she saw the curiosity there. 'You want a beer . . . brandy?'

'I'll settle for a coffee.' Prentice's gaze lingered, accusingly Dani thought, on the brandy glass at her side. 'You want me to make it?'

'I'll do it. You be nice to Dani. She's had a hard day.'

Dani had to resist an inclination to scream. Why did Brian have to put on such an innocent act? Why did he have to walk away from them with such a smug grin on his face? Demurely, she continued to eat her omelette while Prentice stood by the Welsh dresser and seemed lost in his own thoughts.

Dani wondered if he was thinking that perhaps he had interrupted a very cosy, very intimate scene. Brian had denied that, but maybe Prentice did not believe him. Here she was, sitting on Brian's bed, wearing one of his cardigans, without her shoes on and eating an omelette. Very domestic. Her dress was crumpled and her hair was untidy, but maybe that would just make her look even more relaxed and uncaring. Inside she shivered.

'Did you enjoy yourself at the fête, Prentice?' Brian called.

'No,' Prentice answered him, 'not much.' Dani raised an enquiring eyebrow, but he was not looking at her. 'Village fêtes aren't really my idea of entertainment.'

'Too parochial for you?' Dani asked softly. His eyes met hers and accepted her challenge.

'Precisely,' he said smoothly. 'I couldn't have put it better myself.'

'Did Dani tell you that she was divorced?' Brian sang out from the kitchen, and she felt her fingers close convulsively around her fork. How dare he? How dare he make such an obvious and ill-timed remark! How dare he interfere in her life!

'No, she didn't.' Prentice had been lounging against the dresser. He straightened up and thrust his hands deep into the pockets of his cords. He looked directly at her and Dani watched him solemnly for a moment before looking down at her plate again. 'Recently?' he asked.

'No.' She did not feel she had to go into an elaborate explanation.

'Do you have any children?'

'No.'

'You must have been very young.' The statement was made without any hint of gentleness or understanding. Dani raised her head proudly.

'Yes,' she admitted clearly, 'I was. So was he.' And that was all she was prepared to say. He could think what he liked. She would not try to gain his sympathy by telling him that Keith had loved the girl he met in the summer, and that one year later, their marriage had died quietly and painfully.

'Maybe you should have tried a little harder.'

That was unforgivable. Dani put her plate down with a clatter and swung her feet to the floor. She wondered vaguely, as she hunted for her shoes, if maybe the warmth she thought she had glimpsed in Prentice had been assumed and that this unfeeling coldness was the real man.

'You're going?' He did not seem surprised.

'Yes, I'm going.' Her omelette was only half-eaten, but she did not intend to stay and finish it. 'There's nothing I like less than people who make stupid, cruel statements about things they don't understand.' It was, she considered, a dignified sentence, but in her tiredness and anger, she could not be content to leave it there. 'Since you've never been married, I can hardly believe you're an expert on the subject.' She was pleased with that point, despite the pain in her heart, but when she saw the way his lips tightened into a hard line, she repressed the next words that might have come tumbling out.

'Are you two fighting?' Brian strolled back into the room and asked the question lightly, although Dani saw that his eyes were flicking from one protagonist to the other. 'Really, Prentice, I told you to be nice to Dani.'

Dani doubted that he could have made a crasser statement if he had thought about it for a week. What was he trying to do to her? What were they both trying to do to her? She felt trapped by Brian's bright-eyed, feigned innocence on one side, and by Prentice's disapproval on the other. Suddenly her own flat seemed like a haven and she slipped her shoes on, glad of the extra height they gave her, and confronted them both coldly.

'I'm tired,' she said quietly. 'I'm going home.'

'You haven't finished your omelette,' Brian pointed out, but his voice seemed suddenly subdued.

'No. Sorry. I just couldn't eat any more.' If she tried, it would choke her. 'Goodnight, Brian.' She nodded to

Prentice, picked up her handbag and stalked to the front door, wearing her dignity as if it was a cloak that could somehow protect her from those compelling eyes that she was sure were following her every step.

'You don't have to go,' Brian said, but she opened the door and looked back at him, making her face into a chill mask that rivalled Prentice's for its impersonality.

'Oh yes, I do,' she retorted. 'I can't . . . won't . . . face up to his . . .' She nodded towards Prentice. ' . . . kind of arrogant unpleasantness.'

'We really must try to keep out of one another's way,' he agreed smoothly, and when she glared at him, he smiled. Not the beautiful smile that she had seen before, but the mirthless grin of a man who was holding his temper.

'We really must,' she confirmed flatly. 'Goodnight.'

Her flat welcomed her, and in a sudden gesture of defiance she took off her shoes again and threw them across the floor. They landed with two separate thuds on the polished wood and she wondered what Prentice and Brian would think when they heard the noise. Let them think what they liked, she was beyond caring. Those words of Prentice's were repeating themselves over and over in her brain and she could not block them out.

'Maybe you should have tried a little harder.' Yes, that's what he had said. Disconsolately, Dani walked over to her shoes and picked them up, her inherent sense of tidiness not allowing her to leave them lying around, but still the words hammered at her until she flopped down on her window-seat overlooking the dark square and made a conscious effort to bring them out into the open and think about them.

Could she have tried harder to make her marriage work?

Exactly one week after her exams were over, she had met Keith. He had been her sun, her moon and her stars. It had been a beautiful summer and she had fallen headlong in love. So had he. Every day of their holidays had been spent together, basking in the heat of the sun and their mutual passion. They had decided to marry immediately, despite protests from both sets of parents, and had rented a flat in the town where their training colleges were located. It had all happened so quickly that now, looking back, Dani could only remember the events in the context of too much happening too soon.

Could she have done more to hold her marriage together? Dani's eyes blurred with tears as painful memories surfaced. There had been so much to cope with! New marriage, new home, work to be done. Neither of them, she knew now, had had the maturity to recognise the difficulties and deal with them.

Love had died in that small flat but yes, Dani told herself, she had tried. She had neglected her work to go out with him, and had tried to understand what he wanted. When she had finally realised that it was his freedom he yearned for, she had given him that, too.

It all flooded back; all the hurt and the worry and the sense of guilt that she had failed herself and Keith and everyone else. Damn Prentice McCulloch! Dani leaned her forehead against the cold glass of the window. She had to look forwards, not backwards. She might regret the past, but it was unchangeable and she must not dwell on it.

She heard the sound of someone coming up the stairs to her flat. Instantly she sat upright and listened to the careful footsteps. Who? Brian coming to see if she was all right? The steps sounded too heavy for a woman. Or, worse, she wondered frantically if it was Prentice himself coming to torment her further with his calm questions that hurt her more than he would ever know.

'Dani?' One word confirmed her worst suspicions. It was Prentice.

She had a choice, she told herself swiftly. She could either see him or pretend that she was in bed and did not intend to answer the door.

'Who is it?' she called, delaying the decision and furious to find that she was trembling. He scared her.

'Prentice. Can I have a word with you?'

She pushed herself off the window-seat and padded to the door.

'What do you want?' she called, her hand on the Yale lock. 'It's late and I'm tired.'

'Just one minute of your time.' His voice sounded smooth but neutral. He obviously did not intend to try and coax her. 'And then I'll leave you in peace.'

It was much too late for that. He had re-awakened old ghosts, dragged out spectres of her past that she did not want to be haunted by again.

'What is it?' She opened the door and stood squarely in the frame, not inviting him to enter.

'I owe you an apology.' In the darkness he was a shadowy figure, but the green eyes gleamed like a cat's. Fractiously, Dani wondered if she would be better able to deal with him if his eyes were closed. They seemed to reach into her soul. 'I shouldn't have spoken the way I did. Your life is your own affair.'

Silence. Dani tipped her head to one side and considered him carefully. Was it really possible that she had once been kissed by him? From the tone of his voice they could have been strangers. Yet the memory of that brief closeness still lingered like an evocative perfume.

'It is, isn't it,' she agreed at last. 'I'm sorry you dis-
approve of me, Prentice, but I can't change what's happened. And I'm the one who has to live with it, not you. So
if you'll excuse me . . .'

'Okay.' His back straightened visibly. 'I've made my
apologies. Brian will be happy, even if you aren't.'

'Brian?' Now he was adding a new twist to the conversation. Dani opened the door wide again, not realising
that the light behind her silhouetted her slim shape and
that there was a matching light of battle in her eyes. 'Did
Brian tell you to come up here?'

'He pointed out my failings.'

'Perhaps it's time somebody did.' The knowledge that
he was not there of his own volition hurt Dani more than
she would have thought possible. Unhappily she lashed
out at him. 'You might do better to think before you speak
sometimes. For all you know, my ex-husband beat me
every night . . .'

'Did he?' His hand stretched out, caught her fingers and
pulled her towards him. 'Did he, Dani?'

His voice was suddenly harsh and there was such
intensity in the question that Dani was taken aback. His
grip hurt, but the obviously simmering anger seemed for
once to be directed not against her but against her ex-
husband. What, Dani wondered, would he do if she said
yes? Would he hold her against him and soothe her and
once again show her the softer side of his nature? For one
moment she was tempted. It would be so nice to be close to
him again, and wonderful to feel that he was being
protective towards her.

She was too honest to speak the lie. Maligning Keith to
gain this man's sympathy was something that she knew
she could not do.

'No,' she said clearly, 'he never did. He was just too young to be married.'

'And what about you, Dani?' He still had not let her go. His fingers were crushing hers, but the discomfort was a focal point on which she could concentrate because he was just too close to her, and if she stretched out her left hand she would be able to touch him; draw one finger along the deep crease in his forehead and smooth away the tension in his face.

'I was too young, too.' She drew a shaky breath. 'I'm sorry, Prentice, but I can't give you a good reason for not disapproving of me, and . . .'

' . . . and it doesn't really matter anyway.' He released her hand and stepped back. 'It isn't important.'

It might have been. Dani sensed that if she had given him a valid reason for the failure of her marriage, valid in his eyes anyway, then he might now be holding her tightly.

'Whatever you say,' she agreed quietly. Her hand was throbbing where he had gripped her fingers, but it was nothing to the small sharp pain inside her that his last words had caused. 'Goodnight, Prentice.'

'Goodnight.' He nodded curtly and turned to go. 'Oh . . .' He turned back, as if he had forgotten something. '. . . these steps of yours aren't safe. I'll get Brian to fix them. I'd hate you to break your neck.'

'Thank you.'

One last exchanged glance that lingered on until Dani involuntarily held her breath with the tension of the silence. What did he want now? Why wasn't he going?

'Oh, hell!' He moved swiftly and Dani found herself enveloped in unyielding arms that pinned her own to her sides and almost lifted her off her feet.

'Don't!' Suddenly she was frightened of him, scared of the pounding pulse of her blood racing through her veins that his touch caused, scared of the man himself and the dark anger that was back in the raggedness of his voice.

'Goodbye, Dani.'

He kissed her. It was a hard, bruising, claiming kiss and Dani moaned as she felt his teeth cut into her lip. One of his arms circled her shoulders, the other her waist, and she was held against him as surely and as implacably as if they had been glued together. She felt the long line of his body against hers, quivered under the terrifying intensity of the embrace, and closed her eyes with the knowledge that he was taking from her without giving anything back. And there was no time to give. He tore himself away, and she shuddered as he raced down her flight of stairs, his footsteps sounding as angry as the man himself had been.

Dani stumbled inside her flat and closed the door, leaning against the wood and touching her tingling lips with questing fingers. If only that kiss could have lasted just a few more seconds. If only she could have been given a chance to match that strange, powerful anger with warmth, then maybe he would have realised that she understood something of his dilemma. He was walking out of her life because she was divorced. His head was ruling his heart.

The sound of the Volvo being started up took her over to the widow on trembling legs, and she was just in time to watch it being driven away through blurred eyes.

She told herself that she had known a crazy, all-consuming love once before. It hadn't worked before, and it couldn't work now. They were better apart.

Yet, despite the brave words, the empty square echoed the desolation in her heart.

CHAPTER SIX

'Hello, Marina, I'm home.' Dani tucked the telephone receiver under her chin and fiddled with the catch of her handbag as she spoke.

'Did you have a good time?'

'Not bad.' Dani surveyed her tanned arms with pride. 'The weather was beautiful and I met some nice people. What's been going on here while I've been away?'

'Nothing much.' Dani could imagine her sister's mind turning back the pages of the last two weeks like a diary. 'Oh, Brian has had an accident . . .'

'Brian? What did he do?'

'He fell off your staircase while he was trying to mend it.'

'Oh no!' Dani had noticed the new treads, the reinforcement of the whole structure and the brand new handrails as she struggled upstairs with her luggage. 'Was he badly hurt?'

'He broke his arm, unfortunately. Someone drove him to hospital and then Prentice took over. He made Brian leave the Barn and go and stay with his father . . .'

'Brian's father is dead,' Dani interrupted.

'No, not Brian's father, Prentice's father. It is confusing, isn't it? Anyway, he's been gone about a week now and I don't know when he's coming back.'

'Oh.' The idea of the flat below her own being empty somehow did not appeal to Dani. She was used to Brian's noise; to the sound of his stereo and the way he sang to himself. He was company even without them seeing one another. 'Any good news?' she asked hopefully.

'Not that I can think of. But I should make sure you keep your door locked. There's been a spate of vandalism around the village. Jimmy Lake had the soft top of his sports car slashed and Les had paint sprayed over his Range Rover. One or two other cars have been damaged, too.'

'Oh lord!' That was bad news. Dani thought of her unprotected Fiesta in the yard outside and realised that she had not even spared it a glance since her return home. After a holiday in Italy, she did not relish the possibility of having to spend money on it.

'Your car is okay,' Marina said reassuringly. 'Harry drove it round here as soon as Brian had his accident. He would have moved Brian's Morgan, too, but he didn't fancy having to push it.'

'Thanks, Marina.'

'My pleasure.'

They talked for a while longer and then Dani put down the receiver and stretched her arms luxuriously above her head. She felt rested and relaxed after her two weeks in the sun, and ready for school to start again in four days' time, but the news of Brian was depressing and suddenly she felt a little flat, as if coming home was somehow an anti-climax.

She had booked a riding lesson for later in the day, so she pottered around in her flat until the time came for her to change and find her riding hat before setting out for the stables.

Leaving her car at the edge of the riding complex, Dani walked down the concrete yard to the archway that would take her into the nerve-centre of the school, and she stood in the opening for a moment and looked around her.

It was a pleasure to see the stable blocks set on three sides of a big square and to watch the horses as they poked their heads out of the stalls. Dani liked the activity that was always such a feature of the place, and yet it was peaceful, too. No rush and hurry here. The presence of the horses seemed to slow the pace of life to a sedate walk, and the clanking of a bucket as it was carried around the square and the movement of some of the horses in the stalls were all a part of Dani's enjoyment.

She went into the tack room, another favourite place of hers with its smell of leather and its neatness. A peg for every bridle and a place for every saddle, all tidily marked with the name of the horse who owned it; Raffles, Dandyman, Sugar, Zed, Tucker and Thunder.

Thunder's saddle and bridle were missing and Dani winced. Thunder again! He was the only horse that had been available, but the very name made her nervous and she had never managed to handle him properly. It was not the horse's fault. She had seen other riders on him and he had behaved perfectly. She was certain that he sensed her nervousness and reacted to it.

'Ah, there you are, Mrs Robertson.' Her instructor, Mary Goss, walked Thunder out of his stall and handed him over to Dani who took his reins and led him to the exercise ring. This was a large area in the middle of the courtyard which was enclosed with ranch-style fencing and had an earth and sand floor. It was big enough to accommodate about eight riders going through their paces, but Dani always had a lesson by herself, not wanting to make mistakes in front of her own pupils, several of whom were already more proficient than she was. It was only really Marina's enthusiasm that kept

Dani trying at all. Marina loved horses and wanted Dani to hack with her.

Efficiently Dani tightened the girth, let down the stirrup leathers and prepared to mount the animal. This was the easy part and she swung herself into the saddle with confidence, sure that Mary would not fault her.

'You twisted the stirrup leather the wrong way,' Mary said calmly.

'Sorry.' Mistake number one.

'All right. Walk on.'

Walking the horse around the perimeter of the fence, Dani listened to Mary's instructions and began to gain a little confidence. Mary was not being quite as critical as she had been on previous occasions and Dani wondered if she was improving. This was, after all, only the fourth time she had been off a leading rein. She relaxed a little and even let her eyes wander around the stableyard while still listening to Mary.

Lord, what a beautiful horse! As Dani began her third circuit and was in a position to see the end of the stables where the tack room was situated, a rider and hunter clip-clopped through the archway and began to walk around the outside of the exercise ring. The horse was a grey, the colour of old pewter, and the set of his head and neck reminded Dani of the traditional knight of a chesspiece. He was a big horse, and his rider was a tall man, and the two together were a joy to look at. In a grey and black hacking jacket, jodhpurs and a black riding hat and boots the man had the kind of casual confidence that Dani yearned for and envied.

They approached one another sedately, the elegant man and his beautiful horse on the outside of the ring, and Dani and her chestnut on the inside. She was about seven yards away when she recognised Prentice McCulloch.

Oh no! Not him! Not now, now of all times when the advantages were all on his side. He was obviously an expert horseman and she was just a raw beginner. Dani felt the traitorous colour begin to burn in her cheeks as the gap closed behind them, and then he was nodding his head to acknowledge her and his eyes, as they passed one another, were alight with mocking interest. Thunder stopped.

'Concentrate please, Mrs Robertson.' Mary Goss was on to her in a flash. 'Get him moving. Walk on.'

Another circuit. Dani tried to ignore the slowly moving grey and get back her earlier confidence, but she was too conscious of being watched, and Mary's comments became more frequent.

'All right, Mrs Robertson, prepare to trot.'

Obediently Dani shortened her reins a little and pressed her knees inwards, while at the same time becoming aware that Prentice had dismounted and was patting his horse. Thunder responded to her signals and she began the rising trot which she had found so difficult in the first few attempts, but now seemed natural and easy.

'Good!' Mary Goss encouraged her and Dani preened, trying to remember all that she had been taught and making a conscious effort to avoid looking at that tall, immaculately clad figure who was now unsaddling his horse in an open stall. She wished that he was not there, but his presence was making her more determined than ever to shine. Thunder was moving well, she felt light and graceful in the saddle, and when she was instructed to cross the ring diagonally, she managed it with another word of praise from her instructor.

For one half of every circuit, Prentice was within her

field of vision, and she saw him turn to look at her every time she passed the open stall where he was working. If only she could get through the lesson without committing some terrible blunder! She made silent promises to Thunder that if he behaved himself, she would bring him carrots on her next visit.

Round and round. Crossing the exercise ring diagonally, bisecting it from top to bottom, Mary Goss seemed determined to perfect every move, and Dani did her best and waited for her luck to run out. This was all going just too well.

On her next circuit she saw that Prentice had closed the stable door and was walking to the tack room with his saddle over his arm. If only he would leave, then Dani knew she could disgrace herself without his green eyes watching her and assessing her.

He did not leave. When he came out of the tack room, he strolled a little way around the ranch fencing and then leaned his elbow on it, putting one foot on the bottom plank of wood and settling down to enjoy himself. Watching her. And as soon as that happened, as soon as she knew, without being able to fool herself, that his attention was on her, things began to go wrong. Thunder slowed to a walk when he was not supposed to, the horse seemed to lose his will to work, and Dani's concentration vanished.

'Shorten your reins, Mrs Robertson. Where do you think you're going, Mrs Robertson? You must make him go where you want to go, Mrs Robertson.' The instructions became sharper now, and with every one, Dani became more and more desperate. She knew she was doing badly. She knew that as fast as she tried to put one fault right, something else was going wrong, and Mary Goss seemed to sense her growing panic. 'All right, Mrs

Robertson. One more circuit and then bring him back to a walk.'

Dani let out her breath in a silent gasp of relief at the command. At last! Even as the thought crossed her mind, Thunder broke into a canter.

She had never cantered before. She was aware of nothing but the sensation of moving faster than she wanted to, and a feeling of utter helplessness and fear.

'Sit back in your saddle.' Mary's voice was supremely confident. 'Sit back in the saddle and pull him up gently . . . gently!' Dani knew that to her instructor, Thunder's mouth was more important than she was, and it was that fact and the calm instructions which steadied her, and she brought her horse back to a trot and then to a walk, breathing deeply and trying to control her fear. As she came within sight of Prentice again, he was inside the ring.

She had not seen him jump the fence, but now he stood perfectly still, eyes intently upon her, and as she drew nearer she had the feeling that he was poised alertly to run towards her. Had he been going to help?

'It's quite all right, Mr McCulloch,' Mary Goss said. 'Mrs Robertson is fine. Walk on.'

Dani came within an inch of stopping the lesson then and there. Her canter had scared her and once again she became nervously aware that Thunder was bigger and more powerful than she was. He could canter again, if he wanted to. It was pride that lifted her chin and made her urge the horse forward, and pride that kept her walking around and then attempting another rising trot, when in reality she wanted to run away and hide in the tack room.

This was no good. She would never be able to go hacking with Marina. They would never let her out of the exercise ring, and she would not blame them.

'Turn your horse into the middle of the ring, Mrs Robertson.'

Please, Dani begged silently, not those exercises! Not today! Not with him looking!

'Whenever you're ready.' Mary Goss was smiling and Dani heaved a resigned sigh, lifted her right leg over the neck of the horse so that she was sitting sideways, then swung her left leg over the cantle so that she was sitting the wrong way around. Two more ninety degree turns brought her back into the saddle again, and also gave her a good view of Prentice. He was grinning broadly.

'Once again, Mrs Robertson.'

Every time Mary Goss mentioned her name, Dani wondered if it reminded Prentice of their last meeting. She had seen him since, of course, but only at a distance, either in his Volvo or on the other side of the street. They had acknowledged one another, but that was all. She had tried to shut him out of her mind, but that was impossible even though she knew that time could change nothing for them. She was still Mrs Robertson and she always would be. Resignedly she repeated the manoeuvre and caught sight of Prentice with his back to her. His shoulders were shaking.

Dani was shaking, too, but inside where it did not show. Her legs felt weak and every glance at that tall figure made the tremors begin again. The riding outfit suited him so well, emphasising his long, lean legs and the breadth of his shoulders. Dani realised that she was responding to the physical attraction of the man, and that knowledge made her nervousness worse. It was a relief to be told that she could dismount.

The dismount was flawlessly performed according to the textbook. Dani executed it gracefully and earned

herself a word of praise, but when she walked Thunder
back to his stall, she kept him between herself and Prentice and she prayed, quietly and earnestly, that he would
be gone by the time she had finished unsaddling. It
seemed like a small miracle when she walked back to the
tack room and he was nowhere in sight, and she bit her lip
as her heart lurched with disappointment. She didn't
want to see him, she told herself sternly. She did not want
his disapproval like a black cloud over the sun, nor his
presence to bring back hurtful memories.

'Hello.' As she stared around her, torn between wanting to see him and scared of that feeling, he appeared
around the corner.

'Oh. Hello.' Studiously polite, she nodded and smiled.

'I didn't know you rode.' His own voice reflected
nothing but polite interest.

'I don't know that you can call it riding.' She took off
her hat and ran her fingers through her flattened hair.
'I'm not very good at it, I'm afraid.'

'Do you really think you should be off a leading rein?'

She looked directly at him for the first time and saw the
flash of amusement that lurked in his jade eyes.

'It wasn't my idea,' she said honestly. 'I'm not ambi-
tious.'

'So why are you doing it?'

'Marina thought it would be nice if we went riding
together sometimes.'

'I see.' They turned and, by silent agreement, began to
walk back towards Dani's car. 'Well, I think it'll be a
while before you go hacking.' Again there was just a hint
of laughter in his voice. 'You really didn't do too well, did
you?'

His shoulder brushed hers as they walked, and idly

Dani kicked a stone along in front of her with the toe of her wellington boot while she considered an answer. The tone of his voice had been quiet, and there had been no hint of patronage in it, and it would be both unfair and too revealing to accuse him of disturbing her concentration. In addition to all that, what he had said was true; she was not very good.

'I dismounted well,' she said at last, and when he stopped walking and threw back his head and laughed, she was surprised by the spontaneity of his amusement, a little disconcerted by this sudden change of approach to her, and vaguely irritated by his open acceptance of her lack of skill. It appeared that tact was not among his qualities for the day. 'It isn't that funny!' she said tartly. 'Considering how I felt after that canter, I'm surprised I could get off at all. I was scared.'

'So was I,' he said gently, and they stared at one another.

He was scared? Dani recalled how she had been surprised to see him inside the ring instead of outside it. His reactions had been so fast that she had not even had time to notice that he had moved at all. What would have happened if she had not managed to control her horse? Would he have crossed the arena and stopped Thunder for her?

'Yes, well . . .' She was lost for words. She felt a little glow of warmth that he should be concerned, but a voice inside her brain was telling her not to be such a fool. This man did not care for her because she was a divorced woman and he did not like divorced women. She reminded herself sternly that she did not want involvement with a man like Prentice McCulloch.

'Will you have dinner with me tonight?' He took off his

coat, fitted his finger through the loop at the back to swing it over his shoulder, and began to roll up the sleeves of his shirt. He did not look at her. 'We could go to the Plum-tree.'

The Plumtree was small, exclusive and intimate. Dani blinked at him in surprise and hesitated. She wanted to say yes. More than anything she wanted the chance to dress up for him and enjoy an evening in his company. On the other hand, he was not supposed to like her, and she bit her lip and wondered what his motive was.

'The last time I saw you,' she said quietly, 'you made it fairly plain that you didn't want to know me. At least, that's what I understood. I'd love to have dinner with you . . .' She could make that clear, at least. ' . . . but I don't know why you're asking me.'

'I have to do a prospectus for the country club.' He tapped his riding crop impatiently against his boot and Dani watched the moving muscles in his arm with fascin-ated eyes. 'You know more about the area than I do. I thought you might help me out.' He still was not looking at her.

'Prentice . . .'

'Yes?' At last he met her eyes, and his whole face reflected guileless innocence.

'Oh, nothing.' She was bewildered. A man was inviting her out to dinner and she was questioning his motives instead of accepting and thanking him. Dani knew she had to decide what to do quickly or else seem ungracious.

'I'd love to come,' she said gently. 'Thank you. Of course I'll help you, if I can.'

'I'll look forward to it.' He spoke gravely, but the riding crop stopped its impatient tattoo. 'Eight o'clock suit you?'

'Fine. Oh!' A sudden thought struck her. 'How is Brian?'

'He's fine.' A smile crossed the handsome features. 'Getting to know my father and trying not to be impatient because he can't paint.'

'How long before he comes home?'

'I'm not sure. Why? Do you miss him?' The question came so quickly that Dani frowned.

'It seems awfully quiet without him,' she said with a shrug. 'I'm used to hearing him downstairs.'

'I think it'll be about another week or so.' Prentice turned and began to walk towards the Fiesta, and Dani followed him, lengthening her stride to keep pace with him. 'Are you happy with your stairs now?' he continued abruptly.

'Yes, thank you. What was Brian doing when he fell?'

'I don't know. Something to the handrail, I think.'

'Well . . .' A thought crossed her mind. ' . . . who finished the job, then?' Yet she knew the answer even before he spoke.

'I arranged for someone to deal with it.'

'Thank you.' Dani wondered if she would ever solve the enigma of this awkward man. Impulsively she stretched out her hand and caught his arm, making him stop and look at her. 'You're very kind,' she said simply, and again there was a little pause while they studied one another and Dani felt her heart begin to race as the heat of his skin warmed the palm of her hand.

'I'd hate you to break your neck.' He had said those words before, only the last time in such a way that she had been left in no doubt that the idea gave him some pleasure. Now it was as though he was touching her, running his fingers along her throat and around to the nape of her neck, and Dani had to resist the impulse to move her head as if his fingers were really caressing her skin.

'Was that your horse?' She said the first thing that came into her head and felt the intensity of the moment slip away.

'Yes. I'm keeping him here for a while.'

'I didn't realise you were actually going to be living at the Manor.'

'Just until the place has settled down and I've got it running smoothly. If the country club is a success, I may start another one.'

They reached the car. Dani pulled out her keys from the pocket of her jacket and opened the door.

'I'll see you tonight, then,' she said.

'Eight o'clock.' He raised his hand in salute and turned away and Dani watched him walk up the yard, cross the lane, and stroll up the smaller secondary private road that led to the Manor. No doubt some of his guests would use this drive when they borrowed horses from the stables. He had been right when he had said the country club would bring some money into the village, and yet Dani still could not bring herself to like the idea. She shrugged philosophically and turned away.

The three-piece band was playing quietly in a corner and two couples were circling the pocket-handkerchief dance floor as Dani picked up her menu and studied it while trying desperately to think of something to say.

In the dim light of the restaurant her gold necklace gleamed against her skin, underlining the smooth slenderness of her neck and throat, and the black jersey dress clung to her and emphasised the curves of her body. Dani had been pleased with her reflection in the mirror before she had left her flat, but now her poise was deserting her.

Prentice seemed even more reserved than ever, but Dani did not believe it was shyness or lack of confidence that held him silent. She sensed that he was as acutely aware of her as she was tinglingly conscious of every movement and every word he spoke. She had retreated behind her enormous menu with the wary thought that somehow she must armour herself against the warm depths of his eyes and the curve of his mouth that she now, suddenly, found impossibly sensuous.

'Did Brian say that your name was really Danielle?' he asked suddenly, and she lowered the menu and smiled.

'Yes,' she agreed. 'My mother's French.'

'Really? And your father?'

'Yorkshire born and bred.'

'So how did you get to Suffolk?'

'Well, Marina met Harry and came to live down here, and I thought it would be a good idea to move from Yorkshire when . . .' She stopped. It was ridiculous to be talking about her divorce again. It would just make him crawl further into his shell.

' . . . when you got divorced,' he finished quietly. 'Thanks for reminding me.'

'Prentice—' She leaned across the table to emphasise her point. 'I'm sorry. It's never going to go away, is it? Maybe this was all a big mistake. Why don't you just take me home?'

'Because I don't want to.' His voice was low and a deep crease appeared between his eyebrows.

'What do you want, then?' She felt helpless and the question was out before she could stop it. Unhappily she played with the small posy of flowers in the centre of the table.

'I want to enjoy my dinner with you. I want you to enjoy yourself.' He spoke so quietly that she barely heard
him.

'All right.' She sat back in her chair and reached for the
menu again. 'I'll read this and you can tell me about—
about your horse.'

It was the first thing that came into her mind and she
was not surprised when he chuckled. The low intimacy of
the sound made feathery fingers walk down Dani's back
and she wondered if he could tell from her face how much
she liked hearing him laugh. She retreated hurriedly
behind the menu.

After that it became easier. Prentice seemed to relax
and Dani began to enjoy her evening, too. When, later, he
asked her to dance, she had drunk enough wine to quieten
the inner, warning voice that told her to beware—that this
man was not for her. She nodded happily and preceded
him to the small square set aside for dancing, turning into
his arms without any hesitation.

It was as though she had been waiting all her life for this
moment. Dani wanted to melt into that embrace, to be
held closely as if she was the only girl left in the world, and
to feel his body against her own. The knowledge of what
she wanted scared her, and she held herself erect and
refused to give way to the warmth of her thoughts, keeping
a tiny distance between them with careful precision.

'What's the matter?' His voice was close to her ear and
Dani jumped.

'Nothing,' she replied quietly, but she was glad that her
face was turned towards his shoulder and he could not see
her expression.

'Oh, come on!' His voice was lazy and teasing. 'Relax a
little. I'm not going to bite.' His arm tightened just a

fraction, enough to make her either yield to his strength or have to make a definite gesture to pull back.

Dani surrendered. It was easy and he seemed to want it because his arm closed around her even more firmly and he squeezed her hand.

On a horse he had shown a supple, graceful vigour that had fascinated Dani. Now he moved just as easily to the rhythm of the waltz and she was not really surprised. She doubted that there was anything that Prentice McCulloch could not do well.

How would he make love? No, no, she must not think about that. Yet she remembered how he had looked as he sat up in Brian's bed and how she had wanted to reach out and touch him. The temptation to lay her hand against the tanned skin of his chest and feel his heartbeat had been almost irresistible, and she felt the same magnetism again now that she was in his arms.

Dani sighed inwardly and tried to remember when she had last been so close to a man; not just physically close, but sharing a kind of mental unity, too. She could sense exactly where he was going to move so their steps matched perfectly and she knew, without having any basis for that knowledge, that he was relaxed and enjoying the moment.

'Dani . . .' He sighed the word and she felt him dip his head a little and rest his cheek against hers. ' . . . you are so beautiful.'

It was some kind of surrender. Dani circled her arm further around his shoulder with an unbearable sense of possessiveness and touched the nape of his neck with one tentative finger. There were no words that had to be spoken, they just drifted with the music, engrossed in one another, and Dani smelt the faint tang of sandalwood aftershave, the scent of his herbal shampoo, felt the warmth of his skin against her cheek and melted inwardly. Now she was aware of the contours of his body fitted against hers and it seemed, to her dazed and physically assaulted senses, that they were two halves that had just become one whole, as if they had been made for one another.

Dani dared to hope.

CHAPTER SEVEN

'WOULD you like coffee?' Dani fumbled in her bag for the key to her flat, aware that Prentice was waiting patiently beside her and that his arm around her waist reflected the same possessiveness that she had felt towards him earlier in the evening.

'Yes, please.' He leaned forward and brushed her ear with his lips, and Dani chuckled. It had been a beautiful evening and she could not recall the last time she had felt so happy.

'This is nice.' He walked into the room behind her and shut the door, glancing around him curiously as Dani moved to shut the heavy velvet curtains across the window that looked out on to the square. The action seemed to create an air of intimacy between them, and to heighten the feeling of rapport that had been present ever since their first dance together. Dani was delighted when he began to wander around the room as casually as if he had been doing it for years.

'I'll make the coffee.' She went into the small kitchen and switched on the percolator, not surprised when Prentice joined her a few seconds later and wrapped his arms around her waist, snuggling his face into her neck.

'I hope that bed of yours is comfortable,' he murmured. 'Shall we forget the coffee and . . .'

'And what?' Dani swung around to face him and immediately he released her to place one hand on each side of the work surface behind her, trapping her between his arms.

'Don't be so naïve.' It was the same teasing tone he had used earlier in the evening, but now his smile was faintly mocking. Dani could feel her heart knocking against her rib-cage, and in the sudden ominous quiet of the kitchen, the blood seemed to be pounding in her ears.

'Prentice . . .'

'What?' He leaned forward and kissed the tip of her nose.

'I don't think . . .'

'You don't think what?' His lips touched first one cheek and then the other. Dani pressed herself further back against the work surface and felt it digging into her flesh.

'I think maybe you should go home,' she said, as firmly as she could.

'Go home?' One of the well-defined black eyebrows slid upwards in mocking surprise. 'The evening's only just beginning. Oh,' he smiled knowledgeably, 'is this the standard protest you feel you have to make? Would you like to be persuaded? All right.'

'Prentice!' This time there was a definite warning in her voice, but he only laughed and closed the small gap between them, pressing his body hard against hers and finding her mouth with his own with arrogant ease.

Prentice! She screamed the word inside her head, but her mouth opened under the pressure of his in docile acknowledgement of his superior strength, and her arms encircled his shoulders, ignoring the warnings inside her mind.

Prentice. She said his name again, but this time with an agony of longing waking inside her. He was fire and flame and she was going to get burned if she was not careful.

Careful? How could she be careful with this man claiming her mouth, her body and her heart? How could she be careful when she ached to answer the unspoken passion that was now flaring between them, making her feel hot and cold at the same time.

'No!' She levered her hands between them and turned her face suddenly to one side so that his lips grazed along her jaw. 'Stop it!' She pushed against him with all her strength, feeling the thud of his heartbeat under her hand.

'What's the matter now?' His jade eyes scanned her face, as if he wanted to reach inside her mind and read her thoughts. 'You're behaving like a blushing virgin, and we both know you aren't that.'

'Just what does the fact that I'm divorced . . .' She flung the word at him defiantly. ' . . . have to do with this?'

For a second she thought he hesitated, and the thump of his heart against her palm seemed to echo her own as she struggled to regain her composure. He was like a chameleon, seeming to be able to change his colours to suit the circumstances in which he found himself. Polite and formal with people he did not know, delightfully casual with people he was at ease with, devastatingly attractive to her, and now another facet of his personality was emerging. Prentice the lover. Prentice who wanted something that she knew she did not want to give. At least, not yet, and not like this. She hated the smile of anticipation that she saw on his face, as if he was just waiting for her token protest to slide into capitulation.

'Get out of here!' She was surprised at the anger in her own voice, but anything was better than betraying the hurt she felt inside her. Did she really give the impression that she would go to bed with him at his first suggestion? Did he really believe that of her?

'Temper, temper!' Now he was mocking her, and that smile was twisting wryly. 'You're nearly as bad as me.'

'Only where you're concerned.' It was true. She was an equable person and she knew it. The girl who had pushed him into a duckpond and aroused his anger so many times was not the real Dani Robertson. Yet he was banking the fires of her fury once again with the way he raised one devil's eyebrow, and she had to restrain the impulse to lash out at him, to hurt him as much as he was hurting her, to resort to physical violence before she broke down and cried in his arms.

For once his own temper appeared to be under total control. He looked almost amused as she ran her fingers through her hair distractedly and restrained an impulse to stamp her foot, but she kept her other hand firmly on his chest to try to stop another unwanted kiss, and his heart was still pounding. On the surface he seemed calm, but she was aware that this was a subterfuge. Inside he was not as relaxed as he appeared to be.

'Please go away,' she said calmly, clutching the last remnants of her self-control and holding on desperately. 'I don't—I didn't . . .'

'You didn't what?'

'I invited you in here for a cup of coffee,' she said flatly. 'Just that. If you thought something else, then I'm sorry, but you were wrong.' Grave-faced she watched him steadily, not realising how vulnerable she looked with her hair ruffled and her eyes huge in her pale face.

'What else is a man to think?' He shrugged but let his hands fall to his sides, releasing her from her trap. 'There's that picture downstairs in Brian's studio lying around for anyone to see. Will it be displayed in some gallery somewhere? Damn it, Dani!' For the first time he began to let his awesome temper have freer rein. 'Any man who looks at it will know exactly where you have a birthmark!' She had no birthmark. Tricia, Brian's girl-friend, did. 'If you're willing to let Brian paint you like that, why shouldn't . . .'

'Prentice, please!' A niggling pain was beginning to make itself felt above her left eye. It would only take a few words to dispel this particular argument of his, but that small streak of stubbornness inside Dani—the same small streak that had made her refuse to listen to her parents when they had tried to persuade her not to marry in such a rush—refused to let her tell the truth.

'Dani,' his voice softened dramatically and became silky and tender, 'come here.'

She was confused by the sudden change of mood and she tilted her head to one side as she stared at him, wondering whether he was sorry for what he had said or whether this was just another attempt to get his own way. She tried to equate Prentice McCulloch with the gentle-ness of seduction and failed, sensing rather than knowing that his mood had not really changed.

'No thanks,' she said quietly, and the harsh kitchen light reflected sparks of fire in his hair that matched the glint in his eyes. His mouth curved into a smile.

'Whatever you say.' The words were matched by an elaborate shrug. 'It seems I had the wrong idea.'

'You did,' she agreed woodenly, and she wondered tiredly why she suddenly felt cold and sick inside. She just had not expected this from him. Somehow she had thought he might be different. But no, it seemed that he was not, and it brought back memories of other men who had, through the years, thought that because she was divorced she would be only too happy to go to bed with them after an evening out.

'You're a puzzle, Dani Robertson.' Before she could move, his hand reached out and his fingers trailed a line from her ear around to her throat. 'I've never met anyone quite like you.' Had he really never met a woman who had said no to him before? Dani smiled and the fingers that caressed her throat moved a little lower. 'I wish you'd never married him.' The words were a quiet admission of defeat. 'Why couldn't you have made it work? Or why couldn't you have waited . . .'

'Prentice . . .' She could feel her defences crumbling as she looked into his face and she ached to touch it and ease the frowning uncertainty she saw there. 'This is just no good. I cannot help what's happened in the past, and every time I see you, you can't forget it either. Why don't . . .'

'. . . why don't I just go away and forget all about you?' He swung away from her and she heard the quiet laugh that had no humour in it. 'I've tried. I know you're divorced. I've seen that picture downstairs and I've walked into Brian's flat and seen you sitting on his bed with your shoes off and his jacket around you.' The words that he uttered seemed to make his temper flare again. 'What the hell does my brother mean to you?'

He still would not look at her, but the implication was obvious. Dani felt herself going rigid with anger as she wondered just how long that particular question had been in his mind.

'Brian is a friend,' she said evenly. 'He just happens to be my landlord, too, but that's all.'

'Women like you don't have friends like that.' The sea-green eyes were furious and from the harsh tone of his voice Dani knew that his unpredictable temper was threatening to blow up again. Only this time it would be matched by her own.

'Get out of here!' She spoke the words between her teeth. 'Get out of my life and stay out! I'm tired of being accused. If you really think that, then what are you doing here?'

Unshed tears were burning at the back of her eyes, but she refused to let them fall. Her hands sought the comforting strength of the work top behind her, and she struggled against unleashing any more words. She had told him the truth and he would not, or could not, believe her.

'Please go away.' She sensed that her defeat matched his own. He still would not turn and look at her, and his head was bent as he seemed to be inspecting the toaster that stood on the work surface on the other side of the kitchen.

'All right.' He turned back suddenly and, as she watched nervously, he ran his hand over his face. 'You win.'

'It isn't a question of winning or losing.'

'Isn't it?' He smiled grimly. 'I rather thought it was. I keep thinking I've got a winning trick and you keep trumping my ace.'

Dani had played enough whist to appreciate the simile. He had thought she would go to bed with him, probably relying on his dislike of divorced women to lull him into a belief that he could win her over, and she had foiled him with her obvious and genuine anger.

'I'm sorry you feel like that.' If he thought she had won some kind of victory, then she could afford to be generous. And she did feel sorry; for both of them.

'Oh, you don't have to be.' A crooked, rather endearing

little smile crossed his face. 'It's my fault. I should never have underestimated you.' Once again he came closer and Dani resisted the impulse to move away. 'You're very beautiful.' He reached for her hand and lifted it. 'Beautiful and maddening.' He raised her hand to his lips and Dani caught her breath as, slowly and deliberately, he kissed each one of her fingers. 'One day, Dani-girl . . .' It was only later that she realised he had used Brian's affectionate name for her. ' . . . maybe you and I will be able to say goodnight without shouting at one another.'

He was changing yet again! His voice had dropped to a low whisper and the jade eyes were soft as he combed his fingers through her short hair and then cupped the back of her head with his hand and drew her towards him.

Dani could not resist the lure of the gentleness, and as their bodies fitted tightly together, like a latch dropping into place, his mouth met hers and promised her so much if only she would change her mind. She sighed and swayed toward him and heard the chuckle of laughter deep in his throat, but nothing mattered then but the kiss and his arms around her. Dani closed her eyes.

Later, much later, as she sat in her window-seat in the darkness of her room and watched the rain beating down against the cold glass, she wondered how and why she had still managed to resist him.

Idly she let her finger follow the pattern of one particular raindrop as it weaved an unsteady path towards the window sill, but her mind still saw his face, and the enigmatic expression that had crossed it when she had once more, firmly, told him to go. This time he had accepted what she said and had left almost immediately, and in the hour that had followed, Dani had alternately congratulated herself on her strength of will, and cursed herself for not giving in.

In his arms she had felt alive. His own strength and vibrancy had been like a jolt of electricity, stunning her and vitalising her at the same time. She had felt so safe, cocooned and protected from the world, and yet desire had been there, too. She had wanted him, her body had cried out for him, and yet her brain had overridden it all.

If there had been love . . . Dani sighed and watched her raindrop roll out of sight. Oh yes, if there had been love it might have been very different. Was that why she had finally held back?

Another drop of rain captured her attention and she watched it with curious detachment remembering how, as children, she and Marina had both chosen a raindrop and had raced them down the window. Life had been simple then.

Dani turned her head slightly and her attention was caught by an orange flicker. She stared hard, but it was gone before she could focus her tired eyes on it properly. Perhaps it had been the winking of a car's indicator as it turned on to the Sudbury road. No, there it was again! Dani frowned, narrowing her eyes to try to sharpen her vision, and the orange flicker suddenly became a flame.

Fire! Even as the word crossed Dani's mind, and her brain clicked into gear to register the place where the flame was coming from, Dani was getting to her feet. It was the school, her school, and it was burning.

There was no time for coherent thought. The old school was important to her and it had to be saved. Dani raced for the telephone, still seeing that flame in her mind's eye, and rang the fire brigade. She gave them the details while pulling out the flat running shoes that she used for jogging, and as soon as she put the receiver down again, she opened her front door and plummeted down the stairs, jumping two or three at a time and bringing her heart into her mouth when her foot slipped on the wet wood halfway down.

The pavements were glassy with water from the sudden heavy shower of rain, but Dani ran through the puddles as if they did not exist while her mind checked over the facts and tried to sort out what to do.

Mrs Rowett had to be her first priority. The head teacher of the school lived in a small cottage attached to the actual building. Perhaps she had already been alerted by Rusty, her bright-eyed collie who was the darling of the children, but on the other hand the fire might have started inside the cottage itself. Dani increased her pace, trying to lengthen her stride and grateful for the slight downhill gradient that aided her speed as she pounded over the concrete slabs.

The school was well set back from the main road and the houses and shops that lined the street along which Dani was running impeded her view. It was only when, gasping and sobbing for breath, she caught hold of the pillar that supported the open gate leading to the school and used it to stop her headlong flight and swing into the drive, that she saw the flames again.

They were at the right-hand side of the school, as far as they could be from the cottage on the other end. Now the slope was slightly uphill and Dani took a deep breath and forced her tired legs to carry her up the tarmac drive. It had never seemed so long before. Would she ever get there? Her knees felt rubbery and as she reached the green-painted wood of Mrs Rowett's front door, she did not even have enough breath to shout. She began to beat on it with her fists, and as she did so she heard Rusty bark.

'Mrs—Rowett . . .' Her voice had no strength in it, but her shaking fingers found the bell and she leaned against the stone of the small porch that protected the entrance and tipped her head back to gasp for breath. She kept her finger on the bell and, a moment later, heard footsteps on the stairs inside.

'Dani?' The door opened wide and Emma Rowett, iron-grey hair unusually untidy, stared at her. 'What . . .'

'The school's on fire.' Dani managed the words with difficulty. 'I've—called the—fire brigade . . .'

'All right.' Emma Rowett's reputation for calmness did not desert her. 'I'll tie Rusty up outside and . . .'

Dani waited for no more. Now that Mrs Rowett was safe, she could concentrate on the school itself. Maybe some of the records, her own logbook of the children's progress, and correspondence files could be saved.

There was a door leading from the staffroom to the playground around the back of the building. Dani ran to it, picking up a fist-sized stone from the rockery of Emma Rowett's garden as she went. Without hesitation she threw it at the glass that made up the top half of the door, and when it shattered she knocked some vicious-looking shards of glass inwards and then reached through for the key.

Dani's legs were still trembling with exertion, and her heart was thudding heavily and sickly with fright, but she struggled to keep her brain clear. She could hear the fire but not see anything, and as she switched on the light it gave her a sense of security not to have the evidence of the flames to scare her from her purpose.

Fighting to keep calm, she opened the filing cabinet and pulled out the more important items, wrapping them in an old anorak that she kept at the school and in the plastic covers from the typewriter and the spirit duplicator. She hoped that the precaution would save them from the rain as she dumped her bundles outside.

When that was done, Dani took a deep breath and glanced around her, noticing for the first time the petty cash box on the floor and the evidence of the splintered wood of the desk drawer. It seemed that a burglary had taken place and she guessed that if she went into the classrooms, she would probably find them vandalised.

What more could she do? Was there anything else that was vital to the school? There were just too many other files to take outside, so she shut the filing cabinet and hoped that if the flames got that far, they might be protected for a while. As she did so, she glanced out of the staffroom door that led to the cloakrooms. Beyond the cloakrooms she could just see, in the darkness, the main hall and the display cabinet that housed the school's trophies.

Dare she risk getting them? Dani bit into her lower lip and stared hungrily at the cabinet. Intrinsically, the cups were worth little; they were valued for the effort and endeavour that had gone into the winning of them. And she wanted them!

Mentally she tried to work out how safe she would be. The fire appeared to have started in the junior classroom. Next to it was the middle classroom that doubled as the room in which the children ate their lunch, and then came the hall. One room between her and the flames, and Dani was sure that the folding doors that separated the middle classroom from the hall were closed. It should be all right.

Deliberately, she schooled herself to take a deep breath,

and then she opened the door and walked quickly through the cloakroom and into the hall. Immediately she felt the heat of the burning building, but she talked to herself calmly as she reached the cabinet and opened it, making an inventory in her mind as she took each trophy out; swimming cup, drama award, internal school cups. Coldly she took a moment to wonder why they had not been touched by the vandals, but there was no time to think about the puzzle now. The cups clanged against one another as she stuffed them into her arms, and all the while she was aware of the heat at her back and the way her lungs were suffering from lack of air.

There, that was all of them! Dani was forced to take another breath, aware that her lungs had not fully recovered from her run, and as she did so the roar of the flames increased and, as she swung round, she saw fire breaking through the door.

Immediately there was smoke. Blinding, choking, killing smoke. Dani inhaled some with the breath she was taking and immediately coughed, turning towards the front door of the school only two paces away. She struggled with the handle, wrenching at it desperately, before her panicked mind told her that it was locked. She fumbled for the key—Hurry up! Her brain screamed the warning—and when it fell from her fingers to land with a metallic tinkle on the floor, the smoke was becoming so thick that her watering eyes could not see it.

The other way! Dani turned, banged into the open door of the trophy cupboard, and recoiled from it with a cry of pain. Her lungs were aching, and for a moment she did not know which way to go as the small passage got hotter, so hot that she knew she had only a matter of moments, to get to safety. On a half-remembered piece of advice, she dropped to her hands and knees and began to crawl awkwardly towards the cloakroom, frantic for air and knowing that in another second she would have to breathe in the smoke-filled atmosphere or collapse from lack of strength.

The fire was right behind her! She expected to be enveloped in flames at any moment, and the short passage had become an alleyway straight to hell. She had no breath to scream, but she pleaded for help inside her head, and doggedly kept crawling forward while the pain in her lungs seared through her. She would have to take another breath and she knew it.

At first she thought the footsteps on the tiles of the cloakroom were a fantasy, conjured up by her fear, but then she heard her name called through the distortion of the billowing smoke. She banged her hand on the floor to try to attract attention and then Prentice was there in front of her, hauling her to her feet, stooping and lifting her over his shoulder as if she was, Dani thought hysterically, an awkward sack of coal. She squeezed her eyes tightly shut and felt herself being carried back into the staffroom and through the door into the open air.

Air. Real, fresh air. She had thought she might never breathe it again. She took great gulps of it, and immediately began to cough, wringing fresh tears from her smoke-irritated eyes with the lung-wrenching depth of them.

Prentice put her down, roughly, and she was bent over double with a paroxysm of choking while his arm held her up and his voice above her head cursed her vividly and fluently.

'. . . going to call an ambulance . . .' she heard him say amid the tirade of abuse.

'No!' She flapped her hand weakly to stop him. 'Be all right—in a minute.'

'You fool!' His voice thundered in her ears. 'You stupid,—stupid—fool!'

'Had—to . . .' Suddenly she realised that she still had the school cups cradled in her left arm and she laughed weakly. She would have to give herself ten out of ten for determination, if nothing else. She stood upright, groaned, and opened her eyes to look into his face. 'The cups.' She held them out towards him. 'Had to—have them. Oh . . .' Another fit of coughing overtook her.

'Cups?' His voice rose in disbelief. 'You nearly got yourself killed over *these*?' The scorn in his voice annoyed Dani.

'School . . . trophies . . .' she managed to choke out.

'I'll buy you a dozen damn cups, if that's what you want!'

'Just want . . . these.'

The coughing died down and she opened her eyes once again and pushed the silverware towards him. He took them, spared them one glance, then his eyes raked over her face.

'You must be insane!' Something, perhaps something in her face, enraged him and white lines appeared around his mouth. 'You could have been killed!' His hand closed around the swimming trophy and lifted it, and intuitively Dani realised that he was about to hurl it from him.

'Don't do that!' She snatched at his arm and gripped his wrist tightly. 'Don't lose your temper!'

'Lose my temper?' He glared down at her. 'I damn near lost more than that!'

'I didn't mean to put you in any danger . . .'

'I wasn't thinking about me!'

'Prentice, please!'

She did not have the strength to force him to lower his arm, but she refused to loosen her grip, and after a moment, in which his arm was taut with tension and his eyes locked with hers and seemed to reach down into her soul, he slowly lowered his arm.

'You're a fool.' His words held no sting and Dani just shook her head. She did not have the strength to argue with him and waited, hoped for the gentleness that she knew lurked inside this man's veneer of hardness. 'Oh, Dani, you are such a fool!' The cups were placed on the ground, his thick anorak was thrown around her shoulders and then suddenly he was holding her tightly, so tightly that she thought her bones would crack with the strength of his grip. One arm encircled her shoulders and the other took possession of her waist, and she slipped her own arms around him and clung on desperately, burying her face against his chest and closing her eyes as memories of her escape flooded her mind with gruesome scenarios of what might have happened. She began to shake.

'Shh.' His hands rubbed her back soothingly. 'You're safe now. Don't think about it.' Yet his voice was still rough as if he, too, was re-living some private nightmare, and his face pressed into her hair gave Dani an indication that he, too, had been afraid.

They stood in silence for a few moments, wordlessly giving and receiving comfort and, wrapped tightly in his arms and clutching him fiercely, Dani trembled with shock and a sudden aching desire to be like this always; held closely in his arms and protected by him.

'Dani!' Emma Rowett called her name and she started, the spell broken completely when Prentice released her and bent to pick up the trophies again.

'We'd better put these somewhere safe.' His voice was completely neutral. 'I'd hate them to get damaged after you went to so much trouble to get them.'

'Yes,' Dani agreed meekly. The anger was back in his voice and she felt too tired and too weak to fight back. 'And I'd better move the files, too.'

'Of course,' he agreed smoothly. 'Then I'll take you home. If you don't sit down soon, you'll fall down.'

'I'm fine.' But her legs felt weak as she followed him around the side of the school furthest from the fire, and the crackling flames and the reddish glow they cast seemed to throw an aura of light around Prentice's stiff-backed figure, turning him into a menacing Mephistophelian character.

With the files and cups safely stowed on the back seat of the Volvo, Dani leaned against the side of the car and shivered despite the thick anorak.

'I'm going to take you home,' Prentice said, his lips close to her ear, talking above the noise of the burning building and the hubbub of the people around them. 'There's nothing you can do here.'

'I can't leave.' She knew that there was nothing more that she could do, but she could not abandon her school now. She began to walk back up the driveway.

'Oh yes, you can.' His hand on her arm was firm. 'The fire brigade will be here at any moment. What's the point in standing here, soaking wet, when there's nothing you can do?'

Practical Prentice. Dani resented the calm, logical tone of the man.

'This is *my* school.' She wrenched her arm away from his grip. 'It may not mean anything to you, but it's my school and . . .' Her voice rose and a group of people close to them turned to stare. ' . . . and I can't walk away and leave it now.' She made a conscious effort to lower her tone. 'But no one's asking you to stay.' She hunched her shoulders inside her coat—his coat—and took a deliberate step away from him to stand in isolated misery on the side of the drive. Moments later she watched with dull eyes as the first fire engine rattled up the tarmac.

Dani had the sense of walking in a nightmare. So much had happened within a few minutes that she could not accept the reality of the situation. She felt frightened by the power of the flames, angered by her own helplessness, and she thrust her hands deep into the pockets of the anorak and clenched them into two hot fists to try to stop herself from trembling.

'You win.' Prentice's voice made her start. She had thought he had gone. 'We'll stay.'

'You don't have to.' Only a short while ago she had been dancing with this man and loving the closeness between them. Now she resented him, estranged from him by his inability to understand her distress.

'I know I don't,' he answered her honestly. 'But someone has to make sure you don't do anything else stupid.'

'I'm touched by your concern.'

'I thought you would be.'

He stood close behind her, a bulwark against the other people milling around them, and Dani clenched her fists even more tightly as she fought against turning her face into his chest and crying out her shock and unhappiness.

'Oh no!' She groaned out her dismay as the old school bell that hung in its own small wooden belfry and was still rung punctually every morning at eight fifty-five, toppled slowly sideways and disappeared with a crash and a shower of sparks through the burning roof.

Around her she heard murmurs of regret that matched her own, and she blinked back the stinging tears. It had been considered such an honour to ring that bell. The children vied for the favour and Dani herself had known a great sense of satisfaction on the few occasions she had performed the duty herself, and heard the melodic clang of the clapper against the metal. Somehow it was the end of everything.

'I'm sorry,' Prentice said quietly.

Dani shook her head, not daring to trust her voice, but when his arms slid around her waist and drew her gently backwards, she left the support of the stone wall she had been leaning against and let her body relax into his embrace. He might not understand her sorrow, might not have any sympathy for what she was feeling, but he would not let her down. She could trust him and draw on his strength. Dani sighed and closed her eyes for a moment to block out the people and the flames. Perhaps she would wake up and find it was all a dream.

'Let me take you home now.' This time he was asking her, not commanding her, and Dani nodded. She could see that the fire was under control and suddenly she was very cold. Without another word being spoken, they turned their backs on the school and walked to the car, and Dani was grateful for the long, comforting fingers that clasped hers and squeezed reassuringly, and for his silence as they drove the short distance to her flat.

'I feel like a drowned rat,' she murmured as Prentice put on the handbrake and stopped the engine.

'You were nearly a scorched one,' he observed. 'And all for a few . . .'

'Don't start that again!' She shook her head wearily. 'If

I agree that I was a little unwise, can we let the matter drop? Please?'

'Unwise?' She heard the short laugh that was totally unamused and closed her eyes. 'Okay.' Without opening them, she felt him get out of the car, shut and lock the door and then heard his footsteps walking around the front of the vehicle. She felt her own door being opened, blinked her eyelids wearily upwards and took the hand that he was extending. Tiredly she let him lead her up the stairs to her flat and her mental and physical exhaustion would not even allow her to make a protest as he ushered her into the living room and firmly shut the door behind them.

'Get out of your wet clothes and tell me where you keep your drinks,' he said. 'You need a brandy.'

'I don't have any.' She wriggled out of the anorak and laid it carefully over one of her chairs.

'Coffee?'

'Thank you.'

'Dani . . .' She heard his voice die away with a sigh and glanced up into his face. His eyes were as dark as the sea at dusk, his eyelids lowered so that the intensity of his gaze was partially screened from her, but suddenly she was tired no longer. It was as if those compelling eyes were giving her new strength, and she drew in her breath as his stare raked over her, realising that her damp dress was clinging to her body.

'Prentice.' Her voice wavered between a warning and a plea to be swamped by the feelings that were suddenly racing through her body, firing her with a sweet ache that could only be eased by his arms and his mouth. 'Please . . .'

'Please—what?' He came nearer, footsteps silent on her carpet, reminding her of a big cat stalking its prey. The green eyes continued to hypnotise her, his mouth curved into a smile that was half mocking and half amused, and she knew that he understood her dilemma and was waiting to see what she would do.

Dani swayed towards him and the trap sprang. She was in his arms, her mouth captured by his, her body imprisoned by his power and dominated by his determination. Her lips opened beneath the pressure of his and she felt herself bent backwards—reed against the storm—while his mouth urged surrender and would not let her refuse.

'I must save your life more often if this is how you're going to thank me.' He released her lips and nuzzled his face into the side of her neck.

'You didn't . . .' she began.

'Didn't what?' He kept her prisoner within the curve of one arm and leaned back so that he could see her face.

'I could have managed,' she said primly. The short exchange of words was calming her down, allowing her to regain some semblance of control, and she wondered if he had broken the beautiful enthralment deliberately.

'Oh?' The fingers of his right hand trailed down the side of her face. 'Could you? I wonder.' The soft caress stroked her jaw and slid downwards to her throat. 'You haven't even thanked me, you know.'

'Thank you.' Dani repressed a desire to fidget under the gentle stroking.

'You're so very sweet.'

'Even when I push you into duckponds?' If she kept her voice light, maybe she could shake off this wonderful languor that was sliding insidiously through her veins. Not like this, her heart was telling her. He doesn't love you. He'll never love you.

'Even then. Look at me, Dani-girl.'

Reluctantly she raised her eyes to his again, afraid and helpless because she knew what they could do to her. Slowly, delicately, she felt his fingers move down to the small buttons that fastened the top half of her dress, and undo the top one. Then the second button slipped through his fingers, followed by the third, and Dani held her breath and felt herself being torn in two by her raging emotions. Don't! He doesn't love you, one half of her screamed. But I love him, the other half said in a whisper. I love him so much.

His hand parted the top of her dress, the tips of his fingers gliding over her skin with silken caresses while his eyes gauged her response. She felt every touch, every movement of his hand right down into her bones, and she shivered and sighed as the battle raged inside her; wanting and not wanting, loving and fearing, desperate for some sign from him that he cared for her—just a little.

The air was cool on her body, and when he bent his head to kiss her throat she squeezed her eyes tightly shut and let two big tears squeeze their way under her lids. It would be enough, for her, if he told her he loved her and lied. She would believe the lie. But then, as his gentle hand touched and stroked and caressed her body, she let the doubts fall away. She would worry in the morning. The night was for the two of them and for love.

'Damn!' He had raised his head and was looking at her. At the vehement tone Dani flinched and stared at him, the fragile, sensuous mood shattering at the harsh note in his voice. 'Did you have to cry?' He did not bother to disguise his bitterness. 'Do you hate this so much?'

'But . . .'

He shook his head and his lips twisted in contempt. 'I

must have been mad,' he said. 'I really thought that this time . . .' He broke off and shook his head. 'I don't need a martyr, Mrs Robertson. Dry your beautiful eyes and take yourself off to your chaste little bed. I'm not going to touch you.'

'But . . .'

'I thought you wanted this as much as I did!' He was raging now; thin white lines had appeared beside his mouth and his eyebrows were set in a straight, furious line. 'I thought . . . ah hell, it doesn't matter what I thought!'

Prentice swung away from her, every line of his body tense with anger, and before she could even open her mouth to speak to him, the front door of her flat had been dragged open and he had stormed out on to the wooden landing. The door crashed shut with a violence that made the frame shake, and then she heard his footsteps pounding down the stairs.

Dani stood where she was, rooted to the spot with surprise. It was not until she heard the car door slam that she could collect her assaulted senses together and find the strength to move. She ran to the front door, wrenched it open, and stepped out on to the landing.

'Prentice!' Her voice died in her throat as the car engine started.

I love you! She wanted to shout the words down to him, to hurl them defiantly on to his head. What would he do? Would he come back up the stairs again or would he remember that she had been married before and turn away.

She clung to the cold, wet wood of her balcony and watched the car roar away.

'I love you.' She said it so quietly that she barely heard

the words herself. 'I love you. Damn you!' And the stinging rain caught her confession and washed it away into the night.

CHAPTER EIGHT

THE classroom was bright with paper chains, balloons, streamers and a long, painted mural of the Nativity. Dani straightened her back from bending over to watch Cheryl compose a complicated pattern of pieces of wool and twigs and scraps of material into a collage, and smiled complacently.

They had been so lucky. So very lucky. Dani moved a paint pot that teetered dangerously close to the edge of the table and thrust her hands into the pockets of her painting smock as she circled the tables.

Who would have believed that Prentice McCulloch, the day after the fire, would have seen the Managers of the school and the head teacher and put part of the ground floor of the Manor at their disposal? It was such an extraordinarily generous gesture that for a while Dani had suspected his motives, berating herself silently for being arrogant enough to wonder if it was done because she was one of the teachers in the school. She knew it was far more likely to be another idea for improving public relations between himself and the village.

It was not. Just offering the Manor made him a friend of the village people, but he had done more than that. The classrooms were made comfortable and bright with quickly hung curtains, and he was giving up even more of the ground floor so that the school Nativity play and carol service could be staged as usual for the benefit of the parents and the villagers.

Dani loved him for what he had done. She loved him despite everything, but the generosity he had shown had made her proud of him too, so proud that she glowed when people spoke of him with genuine gratitude.

The school occupied three rooms on the ground floor of the Manor; a Manor transformed by the skill of the men working on it so that it maintained its character, but in an enhanced and revitalised form. Dani and Emma Rowett now occupied what had been a sitting room, the library and a music room, all newly painted and the oak panelling carefully restored. They were beautiful rooms and Dani loved teaching in them just as much as the children enjoyed coming up to the Manor for their lessons.

'Mrs Robertson . . .' One of the children demanded her attention and Dani bent over Sharon's picture, admiring the reindeer that the little girl had drawn and giving her another piece of paper so that she could draw a sleigh piled with presents.

The door of her classroom opened, and as Dani turned to see who was coming in, the children also raised their heads expectantly.

'Mrs Robertson—' Prentice walked into the room, followed by another, older man. 'I'm sorry to disturb you . . .'

'That's quite all right, Mr McCulloch.' Dani wondered why he was being so formal. They had kept their distance from one another for almost three months and Prentice had seemed to be away for much of the time, yet on the few occasions when they had met, they had still used their christian names. Dani smiled politely and wiped one finger, smudged with red paint, down her smock.

'This is my father.' Prentice came further into the room and Dani raised an inner eyebrow. So this was what

Prentice would look like as he grew older. Would that russet hair really turn to such a pure whiteness? It was obvious from whom the man she loved had inherited those sea-jade eyes that attracted her so much, and the nose was the same too. But Prentice's wide, sometimes vulnerable, sometimes passionate mouth had to be a legacy from his mother.

'John McCulloch, Mrs Robertson.' The older man stepped forward and held out his hand. Dani shook it, noting the warm strength of it, and returned the smile he bestowed on her with a certain amount of wariness. This was the man with whom Prentice had grown up and from whom, presumably, he had learned his values and his attitude to the world in general; and to divorced women in particular.

'How do you do.' She had to tilt her head back slightly to look into his face. He was taller than his tall son, and broader, and he radiated relaxed confidence. 'Please excuse the children from getting up. They know they mustn't when there's so much paint around.' She gestured to the work tables and hoped that Prentice would appreciate the newspapers spread over the floor to protect it.

'Quite right.' John McCulloch glanced around him and Dani looked at Prentice as he stood slightly behind and to the left of his father. He was smiling and she felt tentacles of love wind themselves more tightly around her heart. Loving him was so difficult. She wanted to reach out and touch him, to tell him how she felt, but she knew it was totally impossible.

'Actually,' John McCulloch continued, 'I really wanted to see all this for myself. I had no idea my son was a philanthropist.' He turned his head, and father and son eyed one another for a moment – there was amusement on the older man's face. 'It isn't like him to . . .' Something in Prentice's face seemed to make him hesitate. 'Well any-way,' he finished, 'I just wanted to look around.'

'The whole village is very grateful to Mr McCulloch,' Dani said smoothly. 'I don't know what we'd have done without him. Certainly the children couldn't be taught in more beautiful surroundings.'

'Its' a lovely old place,' John McCulloch agreed. 'But I shouldn't have liked to have spent a winter in it before Prentice installed central heating.'

'No,' Dani agreed.

'I'm staying over Christmas,' the older man continued. His eye was caught by Sharon's reindeer and he bent to examine it more closely for a minute while Dani saw the information as a useful opening to address Prentice dir-ectly.

'Thank you for your invitation,' she said quietly. 'I'd love to come to your party. I'll write and . . .'

'No need for that,' he interrupted her swiftly. 'I'm glad you can come. I understand a Christmas Eve party was an old tradition before Mrs Desmond became ill.'

'It was.' Dani nodded and turned her attention back to what John McCulloch was saying.

'That's very good, young lady,' the older man was telling the small girl gravely. Then he straightened up and his keen eyes locked with Dani's. 'I understand the chil-dren are putting on a Nativity play in one of the big rooms,' he said. 'I'll look forward to seeing it.' He smiled again and Dani was taken aback by the warmth in his face. It was as if he already liked her, perhaps even approved of her, and she did not understand that sudden grin which made his face look young and boyish. On impulse she moved away from the children so that the two men had to follow her.

'Actually,' she said softly, 'I have a favour to ask, Mr McCulloch.' She looked at Prentice.

'What's that?'

'We need someone to play Father Christmas. Usually one of the Managers of the school does the job, but he can't this year.'

John McCulloch laughed. 'Yes, you do it, Prentice!' he said. His voice dropped conspiratorially as he spoke to Dani again. 'Make sure we get the costume and I'll see he does the job.'

So she really did, as she suspected, have an ally. Dani watched Prentice's eyebrows arch upwards.

'Dad . . .' The word was said warningly.

'It'll do you good,' his father said heartily. 'You get more and more like a crusty old bachelor every day. Too much work and no play, that's your trouble. Frankly, my boy, you're getting boring.'

Was this really the man from whom Prentice had got his prejudice about divorced women? This big, blunt bear of a man who seemed so easy-going was absolutely nothing like the embittered father Dani had expected him to be.

Prentice's lips thinned into an ominously straight line and Dani had to choke back the desire to defend him. He was not boring! He was attractive and vital and she was sure that there was a wealth of warmth inside him if only he would let it out. He had shown her that it was there on rare, too rare, occasions, and she wanted to see it all the time.

'He'll do it,' John McCulloch said confidently. 'Just tell me when and where.'

'Friday,' Dani said quickly before Prentice could step in and categorically refuse the invitation. 'Mr McCulloch, your son . . .' This was confusing. ' . . . has kindly let us have the big room again. We shall have tea and games and Father Christmas usually comes at four.'

'Fine.' The older man nodded. 'And I think you'd better call me Mac. Two McCullochs around is somewhat confusing, and you seem determined not to call my son by his christian name.'

It was not her fault, Dani thought indignantly. Prentice had set the tone of the conversation by using her formal title. She was about to say so when she caught the twinkle in the older man's eye and knew that she was being teased.

'My name's Dani,' she said meekly.

'Good. Well, now that's all settled, Dani, Prentice can show me the rest of the house. It seems a shame to turn it into a country club, doesn't it?'

'Come on, Dad.' Prentice spoke through his teeth, but John McCulloch merely laughed.

'Look forward to seeing you again, Dani,' he said, but after they had gone, she could not forget baleful green eyes that had seen her wry amusement at his discomfiture and resented it. If only those eyes could look at her with love in them. If only.

It was beginning to get dark by the time Dani had cleared her classroom and pegged the children's paintings on a makeshift line to dry. She took off her smock, ran her fingers through her hair and glanced at her watch.

'It's time you were going home,' a familiar voice said from the doorway.

'Hello,' she said casually, swinging round to face Prentice. 'I wondered if I'd see you again today.'

'You did?' He strolled into the room, hands in the pockets of his grey slacks, and Dani turned away to flip through a pile of maths books on her table. She could face him with a third party present, but it was almost impossible when the two of them were alone. The events that had taken place on the night of the fire were as fresh in her mind as the day they had taken place. How could he be so unconcerned?

'Mmm.' She still would not face him. 'I suspect you've come to tell me that you can't be Father Christmas because you have a prior engagement. Right?'

'Wrong.' She heard his footsteps come further into the room. 'I don't like the idea of it, I admit that, and personally I think my Dad would have been the better choice, but I won't back down.' A thread of ruefulness crept into his voice. 'I did suggest to Dad that he should do it, but he just laughed. So it'll have to be me.'

'I see.' Dani wanted to ask what he was doing in her classroom, but was afraid of the answer. She fiddled with her books a second time.

'Don't.' He must have been closer than she had thought. His arm reached around her and his hand came down on top of hers, closing the book. 'Look at me.'

'What do you want?' She smelt the tweedy scent of the cloth of his jacket, and his aftershave, and fought to keep her voice steady.

'I want you to answer a question.' His hand moved to her shoulder and turned her to face him. 'It's quite a simple one.' The green eyes gleamed. 'About a picture of a nude.'

'Oh dear.' She was tired and she did not like the edge in his voice.

'You made a fool out of me.' The words spilled out of

him as if he had been keeping them caged behind his teeth. 'You let me think the woman was you.'

'You seemed to want to think that,' she countered quietly.

'Not true. I hated the idea.'

'How did you find out?' She sensed that he was on the verge of saying more, and tried to distract him.

'I offered to buy it from Brian.' The well-shaped lips twisted into a smile that held no amusement and Prentice shrugged. 'He wanted to know why I wanted a picture of his girl-friend, and I thought he meant you. I got angry. Told him to name his price. He said Tricia would be flattered.' The fingers on Dani's shoulder squeezed painfully. 'You made a fool out of me!' Jade eyes flashed a familiar message of anger.

Dani knew she should have felt relief that the misunderstanding which she had wilfully not explained to him, was now out in the open. She felt nothing but weariness. The revelation had not helped either of them.

'I didn't, you know.' She pulled away from him and picked up the pile of books, holding them closely against her body as if they were a shield that would protect her from this man. 'If you were honest, you might ask yourself if you didn't *want* to believe it was me.'

'Why in hell should I do that?'

'Because I think,' she said carefully, 'that it was easier for you to believe the worst of me rather than the best. Divorced woman posing naked for an artist, maybe sharing the artist's bed. I gave you another good reason not to . . .' Oh no, no, she couldn't go on. She could not, even with her own rising anger, let the word 'love' pass her lips.

'Another good reason not to . . . what?' Every syllable of the question was carefully uttered in a quiet voice that she had never heard before. 'Go on, Mrs Robertson. Tell me exactly what you think.'

'I think the picture just reinforced your prejudice against divorced women.' There was no future for them. What did it matter what she said? 'Why don't you stay away from me?' Her voice rose passionately. 'Why can't you let me get on with my life in peace? Why don't you leave me alone?'

'I can't.'

The soft admission stunned her. He couldn't? Why couldn't he?'

'Prentice, this is silly . . .' she began.

'Isn't it?' A small smile quirked the corners of his mouth. 'I came in here mad as hell because I thought you'd made a fool out of me, and when I see you . . .' The smile widened and made his face soft and vulnerable. 'Well, when I see you, things get back into perspective again.'

'I'm so glad.' She made her voice frosty. 'I can't tell you how tired I get of being around when you lose your temper.'

The smile faded. Dani clasped her books more tightly and took a deep breath. If he could not stay away from her, perhaps she could make sure that he did; sever the silken thread of attraction that linked them with one swift blow.

'You,' he said between his teeth, 'are enough to make any man lose his temper. You think I like to see a woman crying when I'm kissing her? You think I want to believe that you'd allow Brian to put a picture of you, naked, on some studio wall . . .'

'There is nothing wrong with that!'

'. . . for anyone to look at? Why couldn't you have

accepted my offer to find your damn watch gracefully?'

'I didn't know you!'

'Isn't it enough to make any man see red when the lady he . . .' Prentice stopped abruptly. 'When he finds a woman behaving like a fool in a burning building? You think I like being pushed into a duckpond?' The last question was asked on a rising tide of furious indignation. Dani turned away and her shoulders shook.

'Damn!' She heard him utter the expletive sharply. Then his voice dropped. 'Dani, don't cry.' There was the Prentice she loved. 'Damn it, don't cry!'

Hands touched her shoulders gingerly, as if afraid that she might break away and run, and then gripped more firmly. Dani gulped and allowed him to turn her around, squeezing her eyes tightly shut and trying desperately to compose her face.

'You're laughing!' The accusation was full of astonishment. 'I thought . . .' A firm hand tipped her head back and she bit her lip with embarrassment as she was forced to look into his face.

'Sorry,' she said meekly.

'That damn duckpond!' He shook his head. 'I think it has a lot to answer for.'

'You've never forgiven me for it, have you?' She longed to raise her hand and smooth the lines away from his forehead. 'I'm sorry. You were being so arrogant that I couldn't resist it.'

'Arrogant?' His face twisted. 'Thanks. And now I suppose you're going to tell me you asked me to be Father Christmas because you thought I'd make a good job of it.'

'Anyone,' Dani said gently, 'who can make a voice like a dragon, who can do his very best to make puppets come to life for the sake of a few children, will make a very good

Father Christmas.' She trembled against the desire to put her arms around his neck and kiss him. Why, she wondered miserably, couldn't he drop his façade, just a little, and show the world the gentle, compassionate side of his nature?

Prentice McCulloch blushed. Dani saw the red creep into his cheeks, saw from the look in his eyes that he knew he was blushing, and could not resist the little-boy-lost expression on his face. She leaned forward and touched her lips to his, caressing them with gentle sweetness, and trying to tell him with the simple gesture that there was nothing to be embarrassed about. Then she turned, slipping neatly out of the arms that would have restrained her, and walked to the door of the room.

'Dani?' His voice pleaded with her to stay, but she just waved to him as she left the room. If she stayed she would tell him that she loved him, and he would not want to hear that.

CHAPTER NINE

'He's coming!' Darren's high-pitched voice rose above the excited chatter of the other children as they stood at the window of the room in which their party was being held. 'And he's got his sleigh!'

'Now that,' Emma Rowett said softly to Dani, 'is a nice idea. He's a thoughtful man, isn't he? No wonder he wanted the children to watch for him.'

The children's party had been a success. Dani, Emma Rowett and the mothers who had volunteered to do the tea and help with the games, had all worked hard but, Dani decided, it had been worth it. The children's excitement had been reflected in their faces and even some of the older ones, the ones who would be saying goodbye to the school in the summer, had lost their new dignity in being the most senior children in the school and had joined in enthusiastically.

Now they all stood at the big front windows of the Manor and watched as the sleigh, pulled by two ponies, clip-clopped smartly up the long drive. As it drew nearer, they could all hear the jingle of bells and the crunching sound of wheels on the tarmac, and from his place in the sleigh, Father Christmas waved.

'Isn't that pretty,' one of the mothers standing behind Dani said. 'I knew something was going on at the stable this week. They must have converted one of the old carts that was lying around there. Who would have thought . . .'

Her voice died away as Dani glanced over her shoulder, but Dani merely grinned sympathetically. Who would have thought that Prentice McCulloch would have had this amount of imagination in him? Dani looked at the red-swathed figure coming up the drive and fell in love with Prentice all over again. He might be awkward, short-tempered, prejudiced, exasperating and bewildering, but she still loved him without question or reserve.

She had seen him once since their confrontation in the classroom, and Dani still felt warmed by the memory of the children's Nativity play. Prentice had been there with his father and half-brother, and had seemed to enjoy himself. Yet the moment that Dani would never forget— held safe and protected in her heart—had come right at the end when everyone had stood to sing the final carol, and she slipped into the main hall to join in the singing, her duties as stage-manager finished for the moment.

Prentice had stood at the end of one row of chairs, and he had held out his hand to her as she approached. Surprised, she had joined him hesitantly, to be lost in a wave of love for him as he kept her fingers within his as they sang the carol together. It had been a few minutes of precious tenderness for Dani as she had clasped his hand tightly, wishing that their meetings could always be filled with such soft happiness, and when the carol had ended, she had slipped away from him before he could shatter the spell that he had, probably unknowingly, woven around her.

The noise of the children drew Dani abruptly back to the present as the sleigh pulled up outside the front door, and while she hushed them a little, she could not help but be carried away on the crest of their excitement. It was not easy to persuade the children to sit in a large semicircle on the floor to wait for Father Christmas to enter the room, but once they were assembled, Emma Rowett started to sing 'Jingle Bells' in her quiet soprano, and the children joined in eagerly.

Dani looked at their bright faces and sighed, reminded of a daydream that she had enjoyed fleetingly while she had held Prentice's hand and sung the carol. Now it seemed more like a wild fantasy, even embarrassing her a little as she stood among the other mothers. She had dreamed—oh, just for a minute—that one of the children singing the hymn had been their child, hers and Prentice's, and that they were proud parents. A russet-haired boy with green eyes, or a girl who might look a little like her.

As soon as Father Christmas walked in through the door with the big sack on his back, Dani was jolted back to the present, and she could not help a pang of bitter disappointment that Prentice had renegued on his promise. She had expected too much, asked for too much, and this was his answer to the request she had made. Probably, Dani thought painfully, John McCulloch had taken pity on his son and agreed to take his place. This Father Christmas was a round giant of a man, his great white curly beard hiding most of the lower part of his face, and a white wig obscuring his hair. Did Prentice think she could be fooled? Did he really not know that his eyes were one shade deeper and a little more penetrating than his father's? As soon as she saw those eyes, she would know for sure.

When she heard the voice, she smiled. Oh, Prentice! If she could not recognise him, then the children certainly would not know who it was.

'And how are some of my favourite children this afternoon?' He deepened his voice but Dani recognised the timbre of it.

A chatter of excited voices answered him, but the voice of Sharon topped them all.

'Where are your reindeer?'

Dani grinned. She was well used to the awkward questions her children could ask, but how would Prentice deal with this little girl?

'Well.' For an instant he looked up, straight at Dani, and she smiled more widely and raised her eyebrows. Well, Prentice my love, she thought happily, why haven't you brought your reindeer? He had made her love him, so surely two reindeer were not beyond his resources. 'Well, they only come out on Christmas Eve,' Prentice explained. 'You're Sharon, aren't you?' When a wide-eyed nod was his only answer as the little girl seemed awed by the fact that Father Christmas knew her personally, Prentice continued. 'They have so much work to do on Christmas Eve that they stay in Greenland for the rest of the time. Besides . . .' The green eyes twinkled. '. . . it isn't snowing. My reindeer like snow.'

'Will it snow for Christmas?' Another awkward question.

'I haven't decided yet.' Airily Prentice took responsibility for the weather too. 'That'll be a surprise for Christmas Day. Now—I've got some presents here . . .'

Dani had double and triple-checked the contents of his sack the previous evening before taking it into the kitchens of the Manor for Prentice to collect. There was always a dread in her mind that a child would be forgotten or a present mislaid, and there was always one extra present right at the bottom of the hessian bag, just in case.

She leaned back against her wall and marvelled at the

change in her man since his arrival in the village. She felt
her stomach knot as the idea crossed her mind. No, he
wasn't her man. He never would be. Yet he seemed far
removed from the aloof, reserved figure who had crossed
swords with her at Marina's dinner party.

Had he really changed? He was a man of contradic-
tions. He had not wanted to play the part of Father
Christmas, and he had made no pretence of his aversion to
the idea. Yet here he was, with Sharon in his lap, giving
himself whole-heartedly to his role. Dani did not understand it.

The small ceremony continued. Dani was not really
surprised to realise that Prentice knew the name of every
child in the school. It reminded her of the puppet show,
which he had treated with the same kind of thoughtful
earnestness. Would that be the way he would make love to
her? Dani shivered. Would there be careful tenderness or
would he, as she suspected she would, go up in flames at
the first caress. Beneath the civilised, considerate exterior
he had a flaring temper that he tried to smother, but Dani
knew that passion was there, too. Did he have the capability to love as she would like to be loved? Fool! She said the
word to herself angrily. There's no future in it. Not for
either of you.

'Well, I have to be going.' Father Christmas rose slowly
to his feet. 'But before I do, I must say goodbye to your
teachers and to all the people who have helped to get me
here.' Purposefully he advanced on Emma Rowett and
kissed her soundly on both cheeks, and Dani had to avert
her head so that she should not be seen to be laughing.
This was another new facet to his personality that she had
discovered; his capability for impishness. She found it
very endearing.

To the accompanying close interest of the children, Prentice solemnly made his way around the room kissing every adult present, and Dani saw from his actions that she would be the last in line. Suddenly she had no wish for him to kiss her in public. Whatever was between them—if there was anything at all—she wanted it hidden from people, and in his present mood she was not sure of him. Quietly, when his back was turned, she began to edge her way across to a group of mothers standing on the other side of the room, but he turned just as she reached them.

'Mrs Robertson!' His voice boomed across the room. 'Don't you want a kiss from Father Christmas?'

'Go on, Mrs Robertson!' The children took up the call as Dani knew they would, and reluctantly she allowed them to tow her back to where he stood.

'Shy?' He whispered the word as he gravely kissed her on both cheeks and she was torn between vexation and laughter. He could be so totally unpredictable at times. 'Do you think your Mrs Robertson would come home and cook my tea for me while I get all the presents ready for Christmas Day?' He raised his voice and appealed to the children. 'I promise I'll bring her back safely.'

'Oh yes, Mrs Robertson!' Dani found herself and Prentice surrounded by children all urging her to go and cook Father Christmas's meal. 'You'll get a ride in the sleigh,' Darren reminded her, and as she hesitated, not sure whether Prentice really meant the invitation, his hand closed over hers.

'Come on, Mrs Robertson.' Her fingers were tugged, and with some of the children pushing from behind, she was propelled into the hall and then out into the crisp chill of the December afternoon.

'I don't even have a coat!' The idea of a sleigh ride was romantic, but Dani hated to be cold.

'At your service, my lady.' Prentice reached into the sleigh and pulled out a cloak, a rich red in colour and with a thick trimming of white fur around the hood.

'Mrs Christmas!' Someone, some precocious child, started the chant and Dani felt her cheeks flame as Prentice drew it around her shoulders and fastened the clasp that kept it in place.

'Mrs Christmas, indeed,' she muttered, embarrassed that some child could be so accurately have voiced her own thoughts.

'Don't grumble.' There was more than a hint of laughter in his voice, but as he pulled up the hood and framed it around her face, she saw the softness in his eyes and relaxed. 'Come on, Mrs Christmas,' he said, and Dani took his hand to climb into the sleigh, sliding along the bench seat and folding her hands in her lap as she meekly waited for him to join her.

He could drive as well as he could ride. The ponies were turned around and flicked into a smart trot, and Prentice turned and waved as they began to move down the drive.

'Wave, dear,' he said sweetly. 'You inveigled me into this, so the least you can do is to look happy.'

Dani wondered if he really considered that he had been blackmailed into the role he was playing. She felt vaguely disappointed. He had seemed as though he was enjoying himself. She turned in her seat and waved obediently to the children, smiling despite herself at the picture they made gathered in the porch with the light streaming on them.

'You were marvellous!' She turned back in her seat

again as the children receded and Emma Rowett began to usher them indoors. 'You should have been an actor.'

'No, thanks.' He leaned back in his seat a little and pushed his hood back from his head, pulling off the white wig with it. 'Oh God, I'm hot!'

'What on earth are you wearing?'

'My sweaters, Dad's over the top and then Brian's over the top of Dad's. And a thick anorak.'

'No wonder you're hot!'

'Yes. Well, if you're going to do something, you may as well do it properly. Actually . . .' He grinned suddenly. '. . . it wasn't as big an ordeal as I'd thought it might be.'

'I'm glad,' Dani said softly.

'Are you?' He struggled with the beard, peeling it from his jaw. Then he turned to look at her. 'Are you enjoying your ride?'

'Yes, thank you.' Dani answered him sedately, but then saw the way his eyes widened and caught her breath apprehensively. 'What's wrong? she asked.

'Nothing's wrong. You look . . .' He seemed to struggle for the right word. ' . . . wonderful. Come here.'

Obediently she moved closer, and he put one arm around her and snuggled her against him.

'This is nice,' she said softly.

'Are you warm enough?'

'Yes, thank you.'

'My, aren't we polite today!' The mischievousness had not left him. 'Relax, Dani-girl. It's Christmas.' He shook the length of bells that hung beside his seat and began to hum a carol under his breath and Dani, torn between exasperation and amusement, laid her head lightly against his shoulder and swayed with the rhythm of the sleigh.

'And what do you want Father Christmas to bring you this year?' he asked suddenly.

'Snow.' It was the first thing that came into Dani's mind.

'Snow? What on earth do you want snow for?' They had turned off the main drive now and were on the private road that would take them to the stables. Dani watched the bare, leafless trees throwing gaunt branches up to the sky for a few moments and then shrugged.

'Why not? We haven't had snow at Christmas for years.'

'If you could have anything in the world, what would you ask for?' The ponies had slowed their pace to a walk, but Prentice did not seem anxious for them to go any faster.

I want you. She felt like abandoning caution and screaming the words aloud. I'd like to spend the rest of my life with you and making you happy. I'd like to see you laughing with me, sharing things with me, loving me, just being with me.

'I don't know.' She lied quite deliberately. The truth was impossible and she could think of nothing else that would satisfy his curiosity.

'Everyone has a dream, Dani.' His voice softened and deepened dramatically, and the arm around her shoulders tightened. 'What's yours? Tell me.'

Tell him what? That she dreamed of being the wife of a man to whom the word divorced was anathema, bringing back memories of his own motherless childhood? That love, for her, the second time around would be deeper and richer and everlasting? That she could make him happy if only she was given the chance? Perhaps, Dani thought, a measure of the truth would satisfy him and underline once again the differences between them.

'I'd like to get married again some day,' she said quietly. 'I'd like to have children . . .' Now she would get the usual bitterness, the withdrawal from her because she was not what he wanted. She waited to be hurt like a condemned man waited for the guillotine to fall. She had raised the thorny problem again and she saw no reason why his attitude should have changed.

'Dani . . .'

'Mmm?' She cringed from the tirade she thought was coming.

'Am I really so arrogant?'

She smiled at the realisation that the careless word had hurt him.

'Not all the time,' she said softly. 'Just when you get angry.'

'And then I frighten you?'

'Not particularly.' She looked sideways at him. 'What makes you ask that?'

'Just curious.'

No, his anger frightened her much less than the golden flame of love that he had ignited inside her and which refused, steadfastly, to be snuffed out. She realised suddenly that she did want him to make love to her, but that she was scared of failing him in some way. She had lost one love. To lose a second would be devastating. Yes, she admitted to herself, she was afraid. Afraid of loving and losing; of not being good enough; of not being the woman who could make Prentice McCulloch happy.

'Why did you cry that night after the fire?' The unexpected question made her tremble.

'I was tired,' she said.

'And?'

Dani reached for honesty and grasped it firmly. 'If you hadn't lost your temper and stormed out . . . you probably wouldn't have left at all.'

His indrawn breath was a hiss of disbelief. When she turned her head to look at him, he was staring back at her incredulously, and she met his eyes and nodded to confirm her words. The horses skittered fretfully, seeming to sense his emotions as if they had manifested themselves through his hands, and Prentice spoke to them quietly.

Dani turned her head away and stared at the darkness of the oak trees they were passing, shivering as a strong gust of wind whipped across the open land and seemed to strike through her clothes and numb her. It was almost dark now, but she could just see the white-painted gate that would lead them across the road and into the stable yard. What then, she asked herself miserably? Another goodbye? Another misunderstanding born of their uncertainties? She could not bear it.

'When I came here . . .' He seemed to be concentrating all his attention on his driving. ' . . . I didn't realise that I'd be so damn unpopular, even my own half-brother wasn't exactly pleased to see me. The idea of the country club was hated, and once or twice I thought about abandoning the whole thing. But I'm happy here now. My father wants to retire, so we've talked it over and he's going to sell up and come down here to live. I'm staying here, too. I'm buying a small factory near Ipswich . . .'

'Will you be happy with anything small?' Dani regretted the interruption as soon as she had spoken the words, and hoped that he would not ask her how she came to know about his business. Brian had told her that Prentice was a clever and successful executive with his big family company, and Dani had not been surprised by the knowledge.

'It won't be small for long.' He turned to grin at her, and it was the confident smile of a man who knew his own capabilities and liked the challenge of making his ideas work.

They reached the gate, and Dani stayed silent as he checked the road carefully before urging the ponies across it and into the safety of the well-lit stable yard.

'Why are you telling me this?' she asked tentatively.

'Because I want you to know.'

'Yes, but . . .'

'I've got the car here,' he interrupted her smoothly. 'It's too cold for you to walk home.' Prentice brought the ponies to a halt, and as one of the stable girls came out of the tack room and held their heads, he jumped down from his seat, called out a greeting to Mary Goss who was watching them, and walked around to the other side of the sleigh. He held out his arms to Dani. 'Come on,' he urged her, and when she put her hands on his shoulders, he lifted her from her seat.

The action brought their faces very close together and Dani felt his breath caress her cheek as he lowered her to the ground. The fleeting instant of warmth was very precious, but just another reminder of how deeply she was embroiled with him. Everything about Prentice was dear to her, even his temper, and yet they seemed to be drifting apart again.

'I want to talk to you.' His face was close enough to kiss. 'Can we go somewhere quiet?'

The temptation was to say yes, but she guessed they would only finish up by shouting at one another again.

She pulled away from him and he made no attempt to stop her. Facing him squarely, aware that they were being watched, she said calmly;

'Not at the moment. I've got a lot to do.' She cursed her own cowardice.

'Dani-girl . . .' He took her arm and steered her towards the car, and she felt his fingers tight against her arm through the cloth of her cloak and refused to struggle against him in the presence of others. ' . . . I have to talk to you.' His voice held an urgency that she had never heard before. 'We have a lot to straighten out.'

'No, we haven't.' Her foot slipped on an icy cobble and his grip tightened still more. 'Whenever we talk, you always lose your temper. I'm tired of it. All you can see is the wedding ring I used to wear and it's blinding you to everything else. Besides . . .' And this, she thought wretchedly, was the *coup de grâce*. 'I've applied for a teaching post in Yorkshire. There is nothing *to* straighten out.'

CHAPTER TEN

As soon as the fateful words wereuttered, Prentice's body straightened as if an electric current had been passed through it. Dani knew the news was a shock and immediately regretted having told him. It would have been easier just to leave the village quietly without this final confrontation. It would have been easier for both of them.

'Get in the car,' he said quietly.

'I'd rather walk.'

'Get in the damn car!' Every word was spoken with ominous clarity and his grip on her arm had all the crushing strength of a vice. He opened the passenger door of the Volvo and she had no choice but to clamber ungraciously into the seat, staring straight ahead of her as he stalked around to the driver's side, stripping off his red cloak and some of his sweaters as he did so, got in and started the engine, throwing the discarded clothes on to the back seat.

In complete silence he negotiated a three-point turn in the yard, treating the vehicle as if it was a dodgem car rather than a heavy saloon, and then they accelerated out of the gates with a recklessness that made Dani reach for her seat belt in alarm.

She wondered what he thought he was doing, and where he was taking them. He was a capable driver, but the way he was throwing the Volvo around bends, the big headlights eating up the road in front of them, suggested an eighteen-year-old in his first sports car.

'Prentice,' she said calmly, 'if you have to kill yourself with your bad temper, that's your decision, but personally I'd like to live to a ripe old age.' The car was flung around a right-hand bend and Dani held her breath as she felt the back of the car slide. 'Prentice!' There was a hint of panic in her voice. 'What are you doing?'

'I'm sorry.' The speed of the car decreased, dropping down to thirty miles an hour, and as she glanced at the speedometer to check the indicator, Dani saw that Prentice's hands on the steering wheel were shaking slightly. 'Damn!' The word was a condemnation of his own behaviour. 'Dani, I'm sorry.'

'Yes.' Slowly she let out her breath in a silent exhalation of relief. 'Well, since you seem determined not to take me home, we'd better find somewhere to park. There's a picnic area about half a mile along this road.'

The distance was completed in a silence that was thick with confused emotions. Dani turned her head to look out of the passenger window and gradually felt herself begin to relax. Her palms felt sore and she guessed she had dug her nails into them in those few moments of fear.

'Turn here.' She was amazed at the steadiness of her voice. 'Be careful, the ground's rough.'

The big car moved cautiously forward and stopped and then, in a totally unexpected gesture, Prentice wrapped his arms around the steering wheel and rested his forehead on his locked hands.

'Would you mind telling me why you want to leave?' His voice sounded lifeless; flat and unemotional. He raised his head and looked at her. 'I thought you were happy in the village.'

'I was.' In the darkness of the car, Dani could not see his face clearly, but the tone of his voice worried her. 'I think

it's time maybe I had a change. I'm getting too . . .
parochial.' It was a word he had used, so he could not
deny her statement.

'I like you parochial,' he said. 'I'll miss you.'

'I'm sure you'll find someone else to fight with,' she
answered lightly.

'Not easily.' Life was coming back into his voice now.
She could hear a creeping warmth sliding into it. 'Dani
. . . are you really going just because you want a change?'

'That's what I said,' she agreed, but she found that her
fists were clenched again. She did not want to lie to him
more than she had to.

'I'd hate to think it was because of anything I'd said or
done.' He spoke diffidently, as if afraid she might accuse
him of arrogance again. 'Please don't think that I want
you to go. I don't.'

Dani sighed. There was no hint of pleading in the quiet
tones a few feet from her, but she thought she detected a
hint of wistfulness under the formal words.

'I need a change,' she said again, and after that there
was silence as she stared through the windscreen of the car
and felt the bleakness of the view match the way she felt
inside.

There was a small movement next to her, and then his
hand reached over and took her chilled fingers within the
warmth of his clasp. She accepted the gesture and even
squeezed the powerful hand comfortingly, but the silence
stretched on.

Dani wanted to break it, to say something, anything,
that would dispel the tension that was building up in the
car. It made her heart thump uncomfortably, made her
breath come quickly, and drove her mind into a frantic
struggle to guess what his next words might be.

'Tell me about your husband.'

She had not expected questions about Keith. Dani shut her eyes for a moment and leaned her head against the restraint behind her while she wondered what to say.

'Ex-husband,' she corrected Prentice quietly. 'We were divorced several years ago and now he's married again and has a daughter.'

'I didn't know that.'

'Of course you didn't . . . I didn't tell you.' Dani spoke more sharply than she meant to. 'My divorce has always made you angry.'

'I won't be angry now, I promise. Just tell me.'

Was she imagining an urgency in the body that turned towards her, or in the hand that held hers more tightly? Dani trembled and cleared her throat, wondering where she should start and how much she should tell him.

'We were too young.' She had to make that clear. 'It wasn't his fault any more than it was mine. We met between leaving school and starting college. It seemed like a gift from the gods that we should both be going to colleges in the same town. It was like a holiday romance. We'd both finished our exams and we were as free as birds.' Wonderfully carefree days. She could still remember them clearly. 'We fell in love and got married. His parents didn't like it and neither did mine, but we talked them all round.'

'And then?' His voice was unsteady. 'What then, Dani-girl?'

'We did half a term at college before we were married, and then we went back together to a small flat. I suppose, looking back, we had a lot to prove.' Dani wished she could put her arms around him while she spoke. He was such a lonely man and at that moment she knew how he felt. She had never known such a sense of isolation in all her life. 'We had to show them that being married didn't make any difference to our work,' she said simply, 'and for Keith, it didn't. He was brilliant. I wasn't. I struggled but he didn't seem to have to try at all. I think he soon realised that the girl who had been happy to spend all her time with him during the holidays wasn't quite the same girl who had to spend hours and hours working to keep up with the lectures. I think . . .' She flushed painfully in the darkness. '. . . I think I bored him. There was the cooking and the laundry and the housework to do as well, you see. I think he fell in love with the face and not with the girl behind the face. Maybe.'

'Come here.' His voice was rough but she went gladly into his arms, hiding her heated face in his chest. 'I'd call you many things,' he said above her head, 'but boring wouldn't be one of them. Didn't he help you with the chores?'

'No.' Dani pressed her head more closely against him. 'I was only eighteen,' she said unclearly. 'Maybe I was boring . . . then. I've grown up a lot.' The divorce had done that for her. 'We were both just too young.'

'But you did love him?' His arms tightened as if willing her to deny the question.

'I loved the idea of being in love,' Dani said slowly. 'At the time, yes, I thought I loved him. Looking back, the answer would have to be no.' How could it be anything else when she compared her relationship with Keith to the way she felt about this man?

'Dani . . .' Crushed against him, she could hear the heavy slam of his heart. '. . . you've told me how you feel, and now I want to tell you what's on my mind. Do you want to hear?'

'Yes.' Of course she did! This was what she had waited for, hoped for, for so long. 'You must know I do.'

'I'm not used to explaining how I feel.' He stumbled over the words a little. 'It doesn't come easily. All I know is that whatever I'm doing, wherever I go, I see your face. Last thing at night and first thing in the morning, you're on my mind. When I went back home after the fire— remember?—I couldn't settle because you were inside my head all the time. So then I came back to talk to you and I didn't know what to say.'

Dear God, Dani thought helplessly, what do I say to that? What does he expect from me?

'I'm jealous of Keith.' The words were said so quietly that Dani barely heard them.

'But why?' She tipped her head back and tried to see his face in the darkness. 'It's all over. Has been for years.'

'He was your husband.' Prentice seemed to be forcing the words out between clenched teeth. 'He slept with you . . . and made love to you. You've got memories of him that I'd want you to forget.'

His mouth was so close. She would only have to reach up a little and she could kiss him. Dani hesitated, then relaxed, knowing that the words had to be said.

'I can't forget about being married,' she said softly, 'but it's in the past. I don't think about it much.' And that was the best she could offer him. She would not make wild promises that she could not keep.

The inside of the car was getting cold, matching the chill inside Dani's heart. He was sitting so still, as if he was deep in thought and had forgotten about her, and she stirred restlessly in his arms, wanting to bring him back to the Dani that he knew now, rather than the Dani he was seeing inside his head.

'I'm sorry,' he said at last. 'I don't have the right to question you like this.' He shrugged. 'I'm jealous and prejudiced and I've got an appalling temper. They aren't very pretty faults, love.'

Love. He had called her 'love'. Dani's heart skipped and then lurched into a new and exciting beat.

'We've all got faults,' she said mildly. 'Nobody's perfect.'

'Ah yes, but yours are so damn attractive.' He stretched out his arm to switch on the courtesy light and Dani saw a crooked grin, eyes that reflected the brilliance of a precious stone, and a face that softened dramatically into gentle lines. All this she looked at in bewilderment as he tipped her head up, hands cupping her face and pushing her hair back a little. 'I can't resist you!' he breathed, and then he was touching her mouth with his own in a close, lightly clinging kiss that turned her body to flame.

'My love—my beautiful Dani.' He said the words against her lips and his fingers combed through her hair before one hand settled purposefully at the back of her head and the other curled more tightly around her shoulders.

Passionately, unreservedly, Dani gave herself up to his seeking, hungry mouth, wanting to match his ardour, wanting to give him all that he was asking for and more, instinctively stretching up her hand to his neck to hold him more closely against her. This was where she wanted to be; in his arms, pressed against him, showing him that she loved him, drowning in the sensation of those moving lips and the knowledge that she was wanted, perhaps even needed, by this man.

The kiss melded them together, turning them from two people with differing ideas and views into one silent, desiring entity where all that was important was the giving and receiving of love. Dani wanted to cry with the sweetness of it.

It was Prentice who broke the kiss and who, breathing erratically, leaned his head back against the headrest of the car. The jade eyes were hidden from Dani's blurred vision, but he could not conceal his mouth and she knew he was deeply shaken by the mutual flare of their passion.

'Do you know what I'm thinking now?' His voice slurred slightly.

'No. Tell me.' Dani rubbed her cheek contentedly against his chest.

'I'm wondering how many times you kissed Keith like that. If you . . .'

'Don't!'

The brief, idyllic dream that at last they might have found a measure of happiness in the embrace of their bodies vanished with the sharp, jarring crack of shattered glass. Dani pulled herself away from him and sat and stared through the windscreen, horrified by the anger that raged through her, and fighting to prevent the bitter, scalding words of condemnation from tumbling from her lips.

'I think you should take me home.' The words came out flatly and sounded loud in the sudden hush inside the car. Wildly Dani wondered why he had this obsession about her ex-husband. Was she the first woman he had ever kissed or the first woman he had ever made love to? No, of course she wasn't! His mouth and his hands spoke of experience and knowledge. If she was not worried about all the women who had been in his bed, why was he so concerned about the one man who had been in hers? Keith had been her husband, not just a casual affair. Why hadn't he asked if there had been other men in her life?

'I'm sorry,' he said.

'So am I. Please take me home.'

She hoped that he would argue, and she was stunned when he turned off the interior light and started the engine. He had called her 'love', but maybe it was just a word to him. Was it really to end like this? Defeated, Dani slumped in her seat, jostled against the side of the car as it was turned back on to the road, and then staring out into the darkness with dull eyes that kept misting over.

'You know, I have this terrible feeling,' he began quietly, 'that I've made more mistakes in the last fifteen minutes than in the rest of my life put together.'

'I doubt it,' she answered him wearily. 'You've just been honest.'

'I'm not even sure of that.' The car slid to a gentle halt and Prentice turned the engine off. 'Look . . .' He nodded through the front windscreen of the car. ' . . . there's our duckpond. I came out of there thinking that I wanted to wring your neck—after I'd kissed you first.'

'I can walk from here.' Dani got out of the car quickly, surprised that she could move so fast when her legs felt like lead. She could take no more. Not the anger, the jealousy, or the soft words that he had just uttered. He was torturing her with his changing moods, even while she recognised the emotions behind them.

Prentice McCulloch was a lonely man. Brian had said so and Dani believed him. She also suspected that for all his life he had forced his head to rule his heart, and now—maybe for the first time—the loving man inside him was fighting for recognition. And she could not help him. Dani thrust her hands deeply into the two pockets of the bright red cloak and began to walk more quickly away from him.

Footsteps on the path behind her almost made her stop, but she forced her feet to carry her onwards.

'It's a pity it's frozen over.' He loomed up beside her and slid his hand through her arm, nodding towards the duckpond. 'If it wasn't I could return the favour.'

'You could try.'

'Oh lady, that's a challenge!' She was swept up into his arms and she struggled against the powerful embrace as he held her cradled like a child.

'Will you put me down!' she blazed. 'Don't be such a fool!'

'Sorry.' Immediately she was set gently on her feet, but he kept an arm around her shoulders. 'You seem to bring out the worst in me.'

'Then it's just as well I'm leaving.' Immediately she regretted the words. They had been unnecessary and cruel.

'Don't go, Dani-girl.' He swung her around to face him, and his eyebrows were drawn together in a frown. 'Give it just a little longer.'

'Give *what* just a little longer?' she flared back at him. 'I don't understand!' Liar, liar, an inner voice mocked. 'We can't talk without your prejudice getting in the way. Prentice McCulloch, it's time you grew up and decided just what you do want!' Remember the lonely man, that inner voice warned. He can't change overnight.

'Just a child, am I?' The well-loved voice was very soft, with all the threatening quietness of a slumbering volcano. 'Just a kid? You sound like a schoolmarm, Dani Robertson.'

'That's just what I am!'

'A Victorian schoolmarm. Don't treat me like one of your pupils, damn you!'

'Then don't act like one!'

The accusation was unfair and she knew it. Deep inside him there might be a little of the child left, but he was a man. A man from the top of his russet hair to the soles of his feet. She had responded to his maleness that morning when she had found him in Brian's bed, and she had been vitally aware of it ever since.

'I'm sorry.' She took a deep breath. 'I didn't mean that. None of it. At least you're honest enough to . . .'

'To what?' He turned her and began to walk with her towards her flat.

'To tell me how you feel.' His arm was still around her shoulders. They could have been two lovers enjoying the crispness of the night before going home to bed. Only they weren't.

'Did Brian tell you that my parents were divorced?' he asked.

'Yes.' And now he would probably accuse her of gossiping.

'I'm glad. Maybe you can see why . . .'

'Yes,' she interrupted him quietly, 'I think I know what's going on inside your head. I just wish you could see me as a woman instead of a divorcee.'

He was silent after that, and Dani walked with him and listened to their footsteps on the frozen ground and wished she could find the words to help him.

'May I stay with you tonight?' He made the request very steadily and their pace did not falter. 'Father Christmas gets lonely, you know.'

He was nervous. Dani knew it just as she knew what her answer was going to be.

'No,' she said, just as quietly, while her heart cried out against the denial. To be loved by him for just one night—couldn't she give herself that? To hold and be held; to know his passion and give her own desire free rein—couldn't she give herself that? 'No,' she said again. 'I . . . can't.' And with her words, she denied both of them.

His arm around her tightened and she slipped her own arm around his waist to soften the definite words. In the silent village street, she felt as if the world was holding its breath and that the old houses were waiting—as she was—for his reply. Yet she knew he would not be angry.

'I didn't think you would,' he said finally, and this time the silence stayed with them until they reached the stairs to her flat. Then he spoke again. 'Goodnight kiss?' he asked, and his face under the street lamp was vulnerable.

Dani linked her arms around his neck and looked up into his smiling face. She felt that something had been settled between them, but she did not know exactly what it was. She just felt peaceful and happy.

'Why not?' she whispered.

'You turn my world upside-down,' he murmured. 'And I think tonight I may have behaved like the fool you called me. Forgive me?'

'Yes.'

She raised her face for his kiss and closed her eyes as his mouth found hers with tenderness and a muted passion that shook her as much as his earlier anger had. She arched her neck back for more, and he gave more, moving his lips over hers in silent, loving desire that made her bones tremble. His warmth enshrouded her, his mouth promised love, and his arms were both a trap and a haven. When he released her, she felt alone and bereft.

'You'll come to the Manor on Christmas Eve?' he asked. 'You said you would.'

'I'll come,' she murmured. She could still feel the imprint of his lips on hers, as if she had been burned.

'Goodnight, love.'

'Goodnight.'

He turned and walked away. Dani watched him go and knew that she would not be able to accept the teaching post if it was offered to her. She could not leave him. No matter what the future held for them—anguish or happiness—she could not walk away. She kicked at a stone by her feet and it rattled noisily into the gutter. She saw him turn.

'Dani . . .' His voice just reached her. ' . . . this fool loves you!'

'Prentice!' She called his name, but he just waved his hand and kept walking away from her.

CHAPTER ELEVEN

'DANI, you look gorgeous!' Brian stood in the doorway of her flat and appraised her. 'Prentice will . . .' He stopped and grinned.

'Prentice will—what?' Dani picked up her evening bag and arched an eyebrow at the artist.

'Nothing.' Brian was still staring appreciatively. 'I'd like to paint you in that dress,' he continued thoughtfully. 'The shade of green is unusual and I like the cream lace. You look like . . .'

'. . . a Victorian schoolmarm,' Dani finished lightly.

'No. More like a young princess.'

Dani was taken aback by the words and by the sincerity in them, and Brian returned her quizzical glance guilelessly, unnaturally tidy in a dinner jacket with his hair combed and his beard trimmed.

'Careful,' she warned, 'I'm not used to compliments from you.' Yet the words gave her a little confidence. She wanted Prentice to look at her with love in his eyes. She wanted him to see her and no one else in the room, and the thought made her smooth the skirt of the dress with the palm of her hand in a small gesture of excitement.

It was a velvet dress; simple, classical and elegant, the cream-coloured lace at her wrists and throat being echoed by a row of tiny cream-coloured pearl buttons that ran down to her waist. She had chosen it for Prentice, although she guessed he would not realise that the colour matched his eyes.

Brian helped her down the steep stairs from her flat and she stared in surprise at the familiar Volvo.

'Prentice seems to think my old car isn't good enough for his lady,' Brian said, but there was no resentment in his voice. He sounded amused. 'So he sent this over.'

His lady. Had he really said that to Brian? Dani suppressed a quiver of delight and smiled. Yet she was also curious, wondering if Prentice had been talking about her to Brian and if so, what had been said. When she was seated in the big car, she looked across at the artist.

'What has Prentice been saying?'

'Not an awful lot.' Brian snapped his seat belt into place. 'I saw him and his Dad last night and Mac was doing most of the talking.'

'Sounds like a family conference.' Dani reached for her own seat belt and tried not to sound inquisitive.

'Something like that,' Brian admitted. 'I don't think I'd be giving any secrets away if I told you that Prentice hadn't understood all the facts of his parents' divorce. He always thought his mother abandoned him to live with my father. She didn't. She only left Prentice until she and my father could set up home together, and then Mac wouldn't let his son go. He got custody of Prentice and Prentice was too young to remember. Mac set him straight about a lot of things. Things I hadn't known either. From what I gathered, neither of them had sat down and really talked for a number of years. They've always been too busy and Mac didn't realise how much Prentice's attitude to women had been coloured by what happened between his mother and father. Mac was . . . very honest.'

Dani fiddled with the lace at her wrist, nervously aware that the evening was going to be important and wondering what Mac had said to his son. Immediately Brian's big hand covered her restless fingers.

'You'll spoil your dress.' The deep voice was reassuring. 'Don't worry.'

'Prentice . . .' she began hesitantly.

'Prentice is a whole lot of things.' He squeezed her fingers and then returned his hand to the steering wheel. 'Self-contained, confident and single-minded. When he gets an idea into his head, and when he's sure that he's right, he can give himself a lot of problems. But he listened to his father last night,' Brian turned left on to the lane that led to the Manor, 'and he isn't the kind of man to believe he can't make a mistake. You can always rely on him, Dani. I promise you that.'

It was a good testimonial to the man she loved, and Dani knew that Brian was telling the truth. It gave her hope. Prentice had said he loved her—had said it and then walked away as if the words had scared him as much as they had thrilled her. Now, tonight, she knew that all the uncertainties would be resolved and perhaps she would get a chance to ask him why he had left her when, if he had just lifted one finger, she would have run down the street to throw herself into his arms.

'Here we are.' Brian turned into the drive of the big house and Dani caught her breath on a gasp of wonder.

The Manor was alive again. It looked so beautiful, as if all the decay and the shabbiness had been swept away and the old place was proud of itself again. Coloured lanterns were strung along the trees on each side of the drive, and these led her eyes to the house itself, blazing with lights from almost every window, triumphant in its re-birth. It seemed to be holding out its arms in welcome to her. The two great cedars and the immaculate lawns sparkled with the frost that had lain on the ground for several days, and the stars were a bright and compelling backdrop in the clear sky.

'It's so beautiful,' Dani said softly. 'Just like a Christmas card. All it needs is some people standing outside the front door singing carols with one of those old-fashioned lanterns.'

'It is pretty,' Brian agreed. 'I'm glad you like it. The way this place looks now, we should be arriving in a coach-and-four.' He slowed the car down almost to walking pace. 'My brother has some very traditional ideas.'

The great holly wreath on the front door confirmed that opinion, and as Dani and Brian approached it, Mac appeared to greet them.

'This is what I call a real Christmas!' His eyes ran over Dani from head to foot and then the boyish grin that had so endeared him to her on their first meeting crossed his face. 'Come in, both of you. Danielle, you look beautiful.'

'Thank you.' Unused to being called by her full name, Dani suddenly felt shy, overwhelmed by the two big men on either side of her, both of whom were treating her like a highly-honoured guest. Bemused, aware that they were smiling at one another over the top of her head as if sharing some secret, Dani walked into the hall and allowed herself to be directed upstairs to a small suite of a bedroom and bathroom decorated in soft shades of blue. It did not seem like quite the right sort of décor for a country club, and as Dani tidied her hair and stared at her reflection in the glass, her eyes looked back at her with puzzlement lurking in their depths. What was happening? It seemed as though there was some sort of conspiracy going on, some kind of drama in which she was the central character without knowing a word of the play.

It had to be Prentice. He was stage-managing the

evening and as Dani watched herself, a small smile lifted the corners of her mouth and her face softened. He had a flair for the dramatic, this beloved man of hers. What was he planning?

It was with a sense of delicious anticipation that Dani walked slowly along the wide galleried landing to the top of the stairs and gazed downwards. As she had expected, he was waiting for her at the bottom, his head tilted back and the lights in the hall making his russet hair gleam. He smiled and held out his hand to her.

Carefully, step by step, she descended the stairs, conscious that the soft velvet dress accentuated her slenderness and that the lace emphasised the fragility of her wrists and throat. It moved gracefully with her, seeming to give her a dignity that she had never possessed before, and as she came closer to him and saw the look of gentle pride in his eyes, she knew the truth.

Prentice loved her. It was in the green eyes that glowed with the brilliance of the sea with the sun on it. It was in the generous mouth that curved into a welcoming smile, and in the hand stretched out to grasp her own. Most of all, it was in his body that seemed to be swaying towards her, mutely answering her own delight at the sight of him. Dani wanted to put her arms around his neck and hug him, but when she reached the bottom of the stairs she knew that it was not the time or the place.

'Dani.' He took her hand. 'Happy Christmas.'

'Happy Christmas, Prentice.' She allowed herself to be drawn towards him and felt the soft touch of his lips on each of her cheeks in a formal gesture, made intimate by the way a third kiss was laid lightly at the corner of her mouth.

Prentice drew her towards the double doors that led into the principal reception room, and as they stood on the threshold, Dani felt her eyes widen in disbelief as her gaze flickered around it. She acknowledged Marina and Harry and her parents who were staying with them over Christmas, the Vicar and his wife and other people she knew, but it was the room itself that had thrown her off balance. Prentice led her towards a huge log fire that crackled cheerfully in the big, fully restored fireplace, and she gathered her scattered wits enough to speak.

'Prentice—when did you do all this?'

'All what?' He leaned his elbow on the high mantel and grinned at her.

'The last time I saw this room, there was nothing in it!'

'I waved a magic wand.'

'I can't think of another explanation. It's beautiful.'

A thick, cream-coloured carpet covered the floor, and the furniture was a happy mix of old pieces and comfortable chairs. Shades of cream and brown with splashes of orange had transformed the room into a quiet, restful harmony of colour, and the Christmas tree that took up one corner of the room and reached from floor to ceiling added another splash of brightness that echoed the red of the flames of the fire.

'Do you like it?' Prentice glanced around him and Dani thought she detected a hint of smugness in his voice. 'I could hardly have a party without any furniture.'

'I don't understand how you did it all so quickly.'

'My son is inexcusably slow over some things,' Mac's deep voice said at her elbow. 'But when he does decide to do something, it's extremely tiring trying to keep up with him.'

'Did I wear you out, Dad?' Prentice's eyes were alight with amusement.

'I'm not all that old, boy.' Mac patted his son's back and turned away.

Dani accepted a glass of punch but was afraid to drink it. She felt light-headed already, unable to concentrate on the conversation of the people around her, and aware only of Prentice's arm casually yet possessively around her waist, and of his presence at her side. He seemed relaxed and friendly as he talked to the people around him, but somehow she knew that he was as vitally aware of her as she was of him.

Now that she had grown more used to seeing the room furnished, she began to notice the small things; the shaded lamps that had replaced the old central lights and gave the room a glow of welcoming warmth, the big, gleaming coal scuttle that was now a home for green plants, and the pictures on the wall. Yet the Christmas tree drew her eye again and again. She had never seen such a beautiful giant, and the angel that was perched right at the top had a golden horn which caught the reflection of the lights and seemed to flash with fire.

'I'd like to show you something.' He murmured the words in her ear and when she turned her head to look at him, she saw that her own slowly growing excitement was matched in the depth of his eyes. 'Will you come with me?'

'Of course.' To the ends of the earth, if necessary. She put down her glass and walked with him to the door of the room, aware that eyes followed their progress and that Prentice's arm still encircled her waist, giving her the confidence to know that she was being watched and yet not to feel nervous.

They crossed the hall, and now Dani noticed for the first time the old Indian rugs that covered it as Prentice led her into what would be the music room, but which was currently Emma Rowett's classroom. Propped against the wall on one of the desks lay a covered canvas.

'What's that?' She nodded towards it. 'It isn't . . .'

'No, it is not!' Prentice left her and walked over to the picture. 'Stay there, will you?' One flick of his wrist removed the cover and Dani looked at her own face and blinked. She had not realised that Brian's portrait of her was finished.

'Oh,' she said weakly.

'Early Christmas present from my brother.' Prentice was smiling, but his eyes watched her intently. 'Do you like it?'

'Well . . .' Dani did not know what to say. The likeness was there, but how could she be constructive about her own face? Were her features really so delicate and did her hair really heighten the air of fragility that the artist seemed to have bestowed on her?

'Brian doesn't think it's very good.' Prentice left the picture and came to stand at her side. 'He told me to tell you that he'd like to paint you again . . . now that you're in love. Are you in love, Dani?'

'Prentice, please!' She murmured the words and did not dare to look at him.

'I asked you a question.' He was not touching her, but his tension vibrated between them like a plucked bow-string. 'This isn't a game, my Dani. I need to know. I love you. Do you love me?'

His anxious face twisted her heart. 'Yes,' she told him, 'I do.' Her voice wobbled a little. 'Oh, Prentice, I love you so much!'

'I wasn't sure.' Suddenly the man was vulnerable, showing her his uncertainty. 'Dani—my love . . .'

He turned, his arms reaching out for her and Dani, seeing the truth of his words in his brilliant eyes, mur- mured incoherently and closed the tiny gap between them, to be held strongly and safely in his embrace. Prentice laid his cheek against hers and his whispered words brought her own arms around his neck in helpless wonder that at last she was where she wanted to be.

'Love you—love you—sweetheart.' His grip tightened for a moment, almost crushing her, and then eased again so that she was held tenderly. 'I love you so damn much!'

'Yes,' she whispered. 'You've said so before. Why did you run away?'

'Didn't run—I walked.' His chuckle was a mixture of ruefulness and happy delight. 'I'm sorry, love.' He hugged her against him for a moment. 'I can explain.' Lightly his lips brushed hers, retreating even as she responded blindly to the caress. 'Look—' his voice sounded suddenly shaky. 'If I start kissing you now, I don't think I'm going to be able to stop. And there are some things I should tell you. Shall we sit down?'

'Here?' Was her life to be decided for her in a classroom?

'It seems appropriate.' He grinned suddenly, a mercurial change of mood that she found disconcerting. 'Just a minute . . .' He pushed the teacher's table against the wall and perched on it, dusting the top with his hand. '. . . come on.' His outstretched hand invited her to join him and she shook her head at his wish to talk to her in a deserted classroom and obediently sat on the desk next to him, relaxing into his embrace as his arm encircled her shoulders.

'You know, Dani,' Prentice began quietly, almost shyly, 'whenever someone says your name, one picture always comes into my mind. You remember the day of the fête?' His fingers trailed lazy circles on her shoulder. 'Well, after that first puppet show, I went to get you a drink and when I came back you were sitting under the tree with the children around you. Remember?' Dani nodded.

'It was one of the most beautiful sights I've ever seen. You in that pretty dress—don't ever throw it away, will you?—with that ridiculous baseball cap perched on the back of your head and your face all sunny and laughing. And that child in your lap as if he belonged there.' Dani felt him kiss the side of her head. 'You looked so young and happy with your skirt spread around you and the sun in your hair that I wanted to laugh and cry at the same time. And then that kid said Mrs Robertson—and I just curled up inside and died. I thought I'd met you too late.'

'You had.' Dani thought of Keith and impulsively reached out for his free hand to hold it tightly.

'Yes, in one sense I had,' he admitted, and the fingers she was holding twisted and clasped her own. 'Hearing that you were divorced somehow made it all worse. You were legally free, but my own prejudice wouldn't accept that fact.'

'I know.'

'Of course you do.' He raised her fingers to his lips and kissed them. 'Well, I talked to my Dad and he told me a lot of things I didn't know,' Prentice laughed unwillingly, 'and a few things I did. Including the fact that I'd be a fool to let you go.'

'I must remember to thank him.' Dani stroked her thumb over Prentice's tanned one and waited patiently, knowing that he wanted to explain all of it to her.

'He made me see that it was as much his fault as my mother's that their marriage hadn't worked. He told me that she had wanted me with her, but that he had refused.'

'You don't have to tell me all this,' Dani murmured.

'Some of it can keep,' he admitted, and in the circle of his arms that now enclosed her, Dani closed her eyes and drifted happily on a cresting wave of contentment, knowing that she would willingly stay as she was and listen to him talking for the whole night, if that was what he wanted. 'But there's one thing I want you to know.' His voice became suddenly urgent. 'I told you I loved you *before* my talk with Dad. Do you understand? It's important.'

Yes, Dani did understand and she nodded, feeling his cheek rub against her hair as she settled more closely against him, loving the way he was laying down his thoughts and actions before her like an intricately woven carpet.

'You'd already turned me down that night,' he said softly. 'I didn't expect anything else. I wanted it all to happen this evening so that I could show you that everything I do is for you, and you alone. I wanted this Christmas Eve to be . . . very special.'

'It is,' Dani whispered.

'I want to show you something else.' He released her and slid off the table, turning to help her stand and then enfolding her gently into his arms again. 'My sweet Dani,' he whispered, and he rocked her as if she was a child. 'Why didn't you go to bed with me that first time I asked you to? Didn't you love me then?'

'Yes, I loved you,' she answered honestly. 'I didn't think you loved me. And I thought it was some kind of trap.'

'It was.' His lips touched her ear and then the side of her neck. 'I was trying to make you fit the image I had of a divorced woman. Someone who would pose in the nude for an artist . . .'

'There's nothing wrong with that!'

'Shh! Don't let's argue. You're right and I was wrong. But if you ever try it, I'll kill you.' His soft tones made a mockery out of the threat. Dani hugged him tighter. 'I want to make up for all the times you got hurt. Will you let me do that?'

'Yes.'

'I got caught out that night,' he continued reflectively. 'That first time I set out to prove you were what I thought you were, but after that damn fire it was different. I wanted you in a different way then. I wanted to protect you . . . hold you safe . . . Dani, you could have been killed!'

'Hush!' Dani reached upwards to turn his face to hers. 'Hush, love.' She tilted her head to invite his kiss, and his mouth took hers hungrily, causing a sweet ache inside her that was only partly assuaged by the way his hands roamed over her back with a beautiful, possessive tenderness.

'Dani-girl . . .' He broke away, and he was breathing deeply as she opened her eyes reluctantly and gazed into his face. '. . . you drive me crazy!'

'I know.' She raised dreamy eyes to his and saw the passion there.

'Damn!' He made an obvious effort to relax, and laughed when he saw her eyebrows raised. 'Sorry,' he apologised. 'I just can't think straight at the moment. Come upstairs.'

Hand in hand they left the classroom and slowly ascended the wide staircase. Dani let her hand run up the banister rail and enjoyed the smooth feel of the wood as she wondered happily what lay in store for her next. She allowed him to guide her along the gallery and into a big, airy room that was painted in a pale ivory colour but which was otherwise totally bare.

'This is the main bedroom.' He closed the door behind them and slipped his arm around her shoulders to take her closer to the window. 'It gets the sun in the morning and it looks out over the lawns.'

'So it does.' Dani could see the frost on the cedar tree winking in the lights from the house. 'It's lovely.'

'It could be,' he agreed. 'Dani, I gave up the idea of turning this place into a country club some time ago. I want this to be my home, and I want you to live here with me. I want to wake up every morning in this room and see your face.'

Suddenly Dani wanted to cry. It was said so quietly yet so passionately that she had this strange, irrational desire to turn her face into his shirt and weep. He was right, it would be the most wonderful moment of each day to wake up every morning in his arms. Yet one niggling thought remained.

'Don't you still have some doubts?' She moved away from him to stand closer to the window, staring out at the frost-covered grass and at the tree that winked and blinked at her. Would she ever stand at this window as Prentice McCulloch's wife? He sounded so sure of himself, but the dream had been with her for a long time and the reality was still a fragile bubble that she did not dare to touch.

'Not any more.' He came up behind her, slid his arms around her waist and drew her back gently against him. 'I did have . . . mostly about my own jealousy and temper. But then I saw you yesterday, when you were coming out of the grocer's shop. You didn't see me, did you? You had a huge basket of shopping in one hand and some kind of plant in the other and you stopped to talk to someone. Do you remember?'

'Yes.' Dani wondered where this was all leading.

'Well, I knew then that I wanted to see you shopping for us.' He laughed softly and then bent his head so that his cheek could rest against hers. 'Isn't that the oddest thing to think of? I wouldn't have rated domesticity very highly in my reasons for wanting to marry anyone, but there I was, wishing that the bottle of wine I could see was for us to share that evening, and that the plant was just what you wanted for the ledge in the kitchen. I can put the past in its place now, love. It doesn't matter any more. But I want a future that belongs to you and me and no one else. Will you marry me, Dani?'

She hung, suspended for a moment in time and space, not wanting the moment to end, wondering if she could have imagined it. Dazedly she stared out over the lawn. Suppose she failed a second time? Suppose she could not make him happy as he deserved to be? The doubts that she had pushed out of her mind on previous occasions and refused to think about now whispered insidiously to her. So much could go wrong, that ugly little voice said. What if . . .

'Dani!' He swung her around to face him, his fingers digging into the soft skin of her arms, but she would not meet his eyes, dropping her gaze to his throat. 'You can't say no! Damn it, I won't let you!' Still she would not answer him. 'Dani . . .' His voice dropped to a low, caressing whisper. ' . . . are you scared? Don't be afraid, my love. I won't push you. If you want more time—if you want to think about it . . .'

'No, I don't want to think about it!' The words flooded out of her. 'Only up until this moment I didn't have any doubts—and now I do.'

'About what?' His hands cupped her face, thumbs stroking the delicate skin over her cheekbones. 'About me? My God, I don't blame you! I don't . . .' The words began to tumble out of him.

'No, not about you.' She had to make that clear. She stretched upwards, drawing her finger along the frown line on his forehead, trying to ease it away, and then she trailed it slowly down the side of his face. 'I love you so much. I . . .' What words could she possibly use to describe how she felt? She had dreamed of this moment, and now that it was here, she could not grasp it with both hands.

'Are you frightened to try again?' Dani felt her heart thump heavily with fear as she nodded. 'Don't be.' He captured one of her hands and held it to his lips. 'You were too young last time. You said so yourself. This time it will be different. I promise you it will.'

There was such conviction in his voice, such confidence in the steady gaze of his green eyes, that Dani relaxed and the doubts were banished as if they had never existed.

'Of course it'll be different,' she said softly, and she smiled at the look of relief that came over his face. 'It's you, isn't it? And you are . . .' She searched for the right words. ' . . . all I've ever wanted. I love you so much.'

'You'll marry me?'

'Oh yes, my love.'

'Dani-girl!' She was enveloped in an embrace that threatened to squeeze the life from her, but she did not care. He loved her, they were going to be married, and this old house—which had seen birth and death and joy and sadness—would see happiness once again. She buried her face into the side of his throat and was content, for just one moment, to be held by him and to listen to his quiet words of love. He was her rock. She could anchor herself to him, be certain of him, and he would never let her down. It was all there; in his words and in the arms that were creating a safe harbour for her against his heart.

'Can we tell the others?' he asked. 'I can't bear to keep this to myself. I want the whole damn world to know.'

'Of course.' She raised her face and his eyes devoured her, alight now with a flame of desire that made Dani quiver with the knowledge that soon, very soon, she would know what it was like to make love with him. He would set her ablaze, consume her with racing, raging fire, lift her to heights of delight that she had never experienced before. Yet, unlike a forest fire, there would be no ashes and, like the phoenix, their love would never die.

Prentice kissed her and quicksilver flashed through her veins at the first light touch of his mouth. Her lips parted for him, offering and wanting and yielding, and his mouth moved passionately and thirstily over hers as if he could never get enough of her, never kiss her enough, and never bear to stop. Tender, greedy, loving and promising, the kiss bonded them together, turning their declarations of love into a golden chain of commitment that made Dani feel happily and contentedly shackled.

Every line of her body moulded itself to his, and she felt his vitality stimulate her nerve-endings until they crackled with energy. He would always be like this; volatile, fiery, and undoubtedly possessive too. Yet Dani suspected that for her sake he would be able to control his temper. Even if he could not, Dani smiled inwardly, well she would learn how to cope with it. Nothing was impossible.

'Look, my love . . .' He raised his head at last and turned her so that they could stand with their arms around each other and gaze out of the window. 'I'd give you the sun, moon and stars if I could, but it seems as if you already have your Christmas present.'

Dani laughed. Her Christmas present was safe within her arms in the shape of a tall, green-eyed man who would be the centre of her world for the rest of her life. And yet she knew what he meant.

'It's snowing,' he said softly and she nodded. It was snowing; great white flakes falling silently and relentlessly towards the ground. It was going to be a white Christmas after all.

Mills & Boon

JULY 1987 HARDBACK TITLES

── ROMANCE ──

Reluctant Wife *Lindsay Armstrong*	2756	0 263 11451 1
Perfect Strangers *Amanda Browning*	2757	0 263 11452 X
Sea Promises *Bethany Campbell*	2758	0 263 11453 8
No Escape *Daphne Clair*	2759	0 263 11454 6
Love's Renewal *Sara Francis*	2760	0 263 11455 4
Touch Me in the Morning *Catherine George*	2761	0 263 11456 2
Substitute Lover *Penny Jordan*	2762	0 263 11457 0
The Wilder Shores of Loving *Madeleine Ker*	2763	0 263 11458 9
Echo of Passion *Charlotte Lamb*	2764	0 263 11459 7
An Impossible Man to Love *Roberta Leigh*	2765	0 263 11460 0
The Doubtful Marriage *Betty Neels*	2766	0 263 11461 9
The Arrangement *Betsy Page*	2767	0 263 11462 7
Man Shy *Valerie Parv*	2768	0 263 11463 5
Entrance to Eden *Sue Peters*	2769	0 263 11464 3
Where Eagles Soar *Emily Spencer*	2770	0 263 11465 1
Pure Temptation *Sara Wood*	2771	0 263 11466 X

MASQUERADE HISTORICAL ROMANCE

An Unquestionable Lady *Rosina Pyatt*	M171	0 263 11525 9
A Wife for Winter Man *Linda Acaster*	M172	0 263 11526 7

TEMPTATION

Desert Rain *Regan Forest*	0 263 11567 4
The Homing Instinct *Elizabeth Glenn*	0 263 11568 2

DOCTOR NURSE ROMANCE

Angel in Disguise *Anna Ramsay*	D89	0 263 11523 2
Theatre of Love *Lydia Balmain*	D90	0 263 11524 0

LARGE PRINT

Promise of the Unicorn *Sara Craven*	151	0 263 11561 5
Surgeon's Affair *Elizabeth Harrison*	152	0 263 11562 3
A Promise to Dishonour *Jessica Steele*	153	0 263 11563 1